"So you did come back?"

The sound of Adam's voice conjured up memories that Kyla had carefully secreted away years before. Not fair, her heart screamed out. Not fair! She should have had some warning.

No amount of willpower could steady the hand that she reached out, or erase the tremor from her voice as she murmured, "Adam."

"My condolences—" he paused almost imperceptibly before going on "—*Mrs. Ferguson*." He dropped her hand, an insolent curl to his lip. "And now...you've come to collect. How long do you intend to stay?"

Kyla felt dizzy with the emotions churning around inside her, but determinedly she stared up at him. "This is my home, Adam, and this is where I want to be...where I intend to bring up my son."

GRACE GREEN, born on a farm and brought up in the Scottish Highlands, says at heart, she's still a country girl. She was a teacher when she married her engineer husband, and after their third daughter arrived, they emigrated to Canada. Her husband's work has taken them to many different places, from the Maritimes to the Queen Charlotte Islands and the Yukon. They are now happily settled in North Vancouver. Not until she read an article on romance writing several years ago did she realize this was what she wanted to do. Now she combines her favorite hobbies—reading, people-watching and scribbling—and her love of nature into doing what she loves best—writing and spinning dreams.

GRACE GREEN

tender betrayal

Harlequin Books

TORONTO • NEW YORK • LONDON
AMSTERDAM • PARIS • SYDNEY • HAMBURG
STOCKHOLM • ATHENS • TOKYO • MILAN

Harlequin Presents first edition December 1990
ISBN 0-373-11323-4

Original hardcover edition published in 1989
by Mills & Boon Limited

CHAPTER ONE

AN EAR-SPLITTING squeal of brakes shattered the gloomy December afternoon as a late-model silver Bentley swung at high speed into the last vacant parking spot adjacent to Glencraig parish kirk. Gold glinted briefly at the driver's wrist as her gloved fingers thrust back the cuff of her sable coat; full red lips twisted in an apprehensive grimace as she saw that it was gone three.

'Damn!'

Sweeping up her handbag from the scarlet leather seat, Kyla Ferguson slid swiftly out of the car, frowning as a sudden gust of wind from the north brought with it the unmistakable smell of snow. With the expensive 'thunk' of the car door echoing in her ears, she half walked, half ran, over the gravelled forecourt and up the shallow flight of stone steps to the three-hundred-year-old sandstone building with its tall spire.

'Am I late?'

Letting the heavy door click shut behind her, she turned breathlessly towards the usher who was walking back into the narthex from the crowded sanctuary. She recognised him, but, though she racked her brain, couldn't recall his name. Impatiently she tossed back her long black hair.

'Not at all, Mrs Ferguson.' His words had a pleasant Highland lilt. 'The funeral service hasn't started yet. Follow me, if you please.'

With a murmur of thanks, Kyla adjusted the Hermès scarf that was loosely knotted at her throat, and, feeling the erratic thrum of her heart against her fingertips, she ordered her racing pulses to calm down. *Everything's going to be all right, you'll see.*

But she had taken only two or three steps along the flag-stoned centre aisle when she became stunningly aware that everything was *not* going to be all right after all. She could sense that heads were turning in her direction, and seconds later the expectant hush of the church was disturbed. . .

'She's back!'

Kyla's stomach muscles clenched reflexively as the anonymous whisper sizzled in her ears. Shocked, accusing, it came from one of the pews to her left, and she had to summon every ounce of her self-countrol not to swivel round and search out its source.

Every instinct screamed at her to run. The staccato click of her heels faltered, echoing her stumbling heart-beats and the indecision that ripped her in two different directions at once.

But only for a moment.

Then, curling her fingers into defensive fists, she began moving forward again.

'She's back. . .' 'She's back. . .' 'She's back. . .'

The announcement of her return was taken up and tossed from pew to pew, hissing through the pine-scented air of the church—as if, she thought bitterly, she had disturbed a nest of sleeping snakes.

She choked down an exclamation of disappointment. What had she expected? That during the five years of her self-imposed exile the people of Glencraig would have forgotten what she had done?

What a fool she had been ever to cherish such a hope!

She knew that every eye would be raking her slim figure, assessing the value of her calf-length fur, her discreetly sparkling jewellery, her fine leather handbag. She knew also that every last detail of her appearance, from the pallor of her oval face to the lines of strain round her mouth, would be tucked carefully away, to be drawn out later at the funeral reception and mulled over between sips of sherry and bites of fruitcake.

'Sit here, Mrs Ferguson. The minister should be coming through in just a minute.'

Kyla slid on to the cushioned seat the usher indicated at the end of the front pew. . .and when he turned to retrace his steps she caught her first glimpse of the heavy mahogany casket, strewn with wreaths of tawny-coloured flowers, that rested below the pulpit.

The sight caught her off guard, and a lump formed in her throat. Quickly she bowed her head and, drawing off her long gloves, fumbled in her bag for a handkerchief. How totally unexpected, that she should ever shed a tear for Barclay Ferguson!

A picture of her father-in-law rose unbidden to her mind: the steel-grey hair, the square jaw, the shrewd blue eyes. . .

Fiercely Kyla dabbed her tears away. She hadn't come home to Glencraig to wallow in the misery of the past, or to resurrect thoughts of what might have been. On the contrary, she had come to fight for the future.

Tucking the crumpled handkerchief back into her bag, she closed the gold catch with a determined snap. What she was going to do wouldn't be easy. It would be painful, and it would be humiliating. But nothing—and nobody—was going to stop her.

Hundreds of tiny invisible hammers pounded her temples, making her head throb as she focused her thoughts on her reason for coming back to this small Scottish town where she had been born. Ever since Drew had died last year, their son Kevin had withdrawn into himself, unable to understand why the father he adored had deserted him. For months now, Kyla had been fighting a losing battle with her conscience. Recollections of her own idyllic childhood had nagged at her unceasingly—memories of her loving family, combined with images of the beautiful countryside around Glencraig. In her heart, she knew that the lonely life she and Kevin were leading in Toronto was less than ideal for the four-year-old. If only she could find the courage to go back to the glen.

And then, on the very day when she'd made up her mind and listed the house with a estate agent, her father-in-law had died. As his chief beneficiary, she had to come home to settle his estate. It had seemed to her a sign that fate approved her decision.

Her eyes misted again as she stared unseeingly at the small pine tree decorating the chancel for the Christmas season. Tomorrow she'd go to Tigh Na Mara, talk to her parents, and ask her sister Nairne to forgive her.

She lowered her gaze to the black gloves which she had unconsciously crushed into a tight ball in her lap. First she had to get through today—the funeral service, the short ceremony at the cemetery, the reception.

Especially the reception. As the new owner of Ferguson Whisky, she would be meeting all the people connected with the company; as the new mistress of Glencraig House, she'd be hostess to all Barclay Ferguson's friends.

She refused to acknowledge the surge of panic that rose inside her. She *knew* that she could do it.

She also knew that it was going to be the second most difficult thing she had ever had to do in her life.

'Still slamming that front door the way you used to when you came calling for Drew years ago, missy. Now that you've got a bairn sleeping upstairs, you'll have to learn to make a noise quietly.'

Kyla whirled round at the foot of the stairs as the shrunken figure of Barclay's housekeeper materialised from the passage leading to the back of Glencraig House. She was wearing a navy cardigan over her stooped shoulders, and a disapproving frown on a small, round face already deeply wrinkled from half a century of heavy smoking.

One nicotine-stained hand smoothed down a springy, smoke-yellowed curl. 'The funeral's over, then? You're the first back?'

Kyla nodded. 'Are you sure he's still sleeping, Martha?' Her eyes anxiously followed the curve of the white-painted banister up to the landing. 'You've kept a good check on him?'

'Aye. But the wee lamb's going to be out like a light till morning.' The housekeeper nodded authoritatively. 'It's that jet lag.'

A teasing chuckle escaped Kyla's lips. 'You'd know all about that, of course, widely travelled as you are!' She was well aware that in all her nearly seventy years Martha Thom had never travelled more than fifty miles from the glen.

'You don't have to murder someone to guess what it'd feel like.' The elderly woman's long green eyes gleamed with sly humour. 'You're still as pert as you used to be, missy!'

'I'd love a quick cuppa in the kitchen before everyone gets here.' Kyla flashed a coaxing grin as she started up the stairs. 'It was bitterly cold at the cemetery.' Reaching the top of the stairs, she called back over her shoulder, 'I shouldn't be surprised if there's a storm on the way.'

As she crossed the well-lit landing to the room where Kevin was sleeping, she heard Martha's voice rise up the stairwell like the disembodied prophecy of an oracle. 'Aye, missy, there's a storm on the way all right. And you're the one that's brought it!'

Kyla paused with her fingers curled round the door-handle. Martha's tone was ominous, as if she were referring not to a storm threatening from the north, but another kind of storn, the kind that disrupted people's lives.

Absurd! She had no intention of disrupting the normally steady pattern of life in Glencraig. Surely Martha would have no reason to imply that she would? With a little shake of her head, she dismissed the notion as she opened the door of Kevin's room.

What little light was left of the winter afternoon had been closed out by heavy velvet curtains. One small lamp glowed pink by the bedside, the room was warm, and the air smelled of the mint-flavoured salve she'd bought for Kevin at the airport for his chapped lips.

She moved quietly across to the bed. With a light brush of her palm, she swept the tousled fair hair back from Kevin's forehead and felt a pang of uneasiness as she noticed the drawn look pulling at the fine, delicate features. Her lips compressed. Dear heaven, she thought, a little child shouldn't know such unhappiness. Blinking back her tears, she tugged the thick woollen blankets up to his chin, and tucked them in cosily. Oh, she was glad she'd come back. Surely her plan was going to work? Surely it wasn't too late?

Wearily she crossed the hall to the large bedroom Martha had prepared for her. Switching on the light, she tugged off her scarf and threw her fur on to the queen-sized bed before making her way to the window. As she raised her hand to draw the royal blue rep curtains, she glanced down, her attention caught by the glare of headlights in the dusk. To her surprise, a car was pulling in at the back door. Strange, she mused—surely the guests would park at the front of the house on such a formal occasion?

Holding the heavy fabric to the side, she watched curiously as a tall figure in a bulky overcoat uncoiled himself from the vehicle and began walking up the paved path. In the half-light it was impossible to distinguish who it was, but as he passed the kitchen window the light from inside played briefly on the upper part of his body. Something stirred in Kyla's heart as she saw the black hair, the broad shoulders, the rangy form.

A flood of emotion surged through her as the figure disappeared, and vaguely she realised that her fingers had curled like frozen claws into the roughly textured rep.

Could she be mistaken? Was there anywhere in the world another man who held himself in that particular way, moving his tall, powerful frame with such easy animal grace?

Legs shaking, Kyla stepped over to the bed, supporting herself by touching the top of the dresser, then the back of a chair as her booted feet stumbled across the carpet. The mattress creaked slightly as she sank on to the edge of the bed. With a tortured groan, she leaned forward, her elbows digging into the flesh of her thighs as she buried her flushed face in the palms of her hands. For five years, till this very moment, she had managed to shut Adam Garvie out of her mind.

'Oh, lord!' she whispered, her voice a despairing sigh in the silence of the large room. 'How am I going to face him?'

For a long time she sat, squeezing back the tears that tried to find a way past her fingertips. Finally she wiped her palms against her eyes and, feeling as if she'd aged ten years in as many minutes, pushed herself up from the bed. She had to go down. There was no way around it.

But she wasn't going to the kitchen. Chances were that he, like herself, wanted a quiet cup of tea with Martha, or—and she felt a shiver of premonition crawl up her spine—with her? Perhaps he wanted to get her on her own, and ask some questions?

Her lower lip was trembling. She rubbed it roughly with the back of her hand. She'd keep away from him. The drawing-room would be crowded with mourners; it shouldn't be too hard to avoid being alone with Adam.

She glanced briefly at her reflection in the dressing-table mirror, grimacing when she saw how the black dress which had fitted her perfectly on the day of Drew's funeral a year ago now hung on her thin frame, making her seem almost gaunt.

As she bent to tug off her high leather boots and slip her narrow feet into a pair of black pumps, she acknowledged with a feeling akin to despair that just one brief glimpse of Adam had been enough to disturb the dreams that she had buried when she'd married Drew.

And she *had* buried them. To marry a man and be in love with someone else was bad enough, but to carry that love into marriage would have been a sin.

And enough sins had already been committed.

The crowded drawing-room, the acrid smell of cigarette smoke, the constant strain of greeting all the guests, had given Kyla a roaring headache. . .

'Thank you for coming. . .' 'Good of you to turn out in such weather. . .' 'Yes, Barclay was a wonderful man. . .'

She had met all Barclay's important friends, all his business colleagues. Now, if the local worthies would only stop their gossiping and go home, she could go upstairs and lie down for a while. She was finding it hard to keep her eyes open.

She slid a surreptitious glance at the ormolu clock on the mantelpiece behind Alexander Gordon's black-suited figure. The lawyer, senior partner of Glencraig's only law firm, Gordon, Gordon and Duff, had been clinging to her like a burr during the past half-hour. The only time he stopped talking was when he was swilling back the neat whisky in his glass. She got the distinct impression that he was one of those sadly misguided males who thought that all young widows were like ripe, succulent peaches, streaming with juice as they waited to be plucked from the tree.

'Barclay's will is quite straightforward, my dear.' He smoothed a well-manicured hand over his carefully brushed salt and pepper hair. His sensual lips glistened as he went on, 'This is Friday. I thought I might come over to the house on Monday morning. We could get started on the paperwork.'

His mouth opened in a wide smile that held no humour. It made Kyla think of a shark about to attack.

'Monday?' Her mind moved quickly. A meeting alone here in the drawing-room might well end up in a frantic chase round the chesterfield. The very possibility made her shiver, as if a spider were crawling down her spine. If they transacted their business in his office, when it was finished she could just get up and leave. . .

'Oh, sorry, Alex. I have to go into town Monday morning.' She paused, and bit her lip as if thinking. 'But actually I'd have time to pop into your office for about half an hour. That would probably be better in any case, as you'd have everything at hand, wouldn't you? Shall we say around ten o'clock?'

His aggressive nose, his sunken cheeks, had an oily sheen that was, Kyla thought, most unattractive.

'Ten o'clock?' He drained the last of the whisky from his glass and smacked his thick lips. 'Yes, that should be all right.'

'Good.' Kyla smiled in a manner she hoped would indicate that their conversation was at an end. The lawyer cleared his throat pompously.

'Now, I won't monopolise you any longer, Kyla, my dear. I think there are still quite a few people here who want to offer their condolences.'

He patted Kyla's arm in a gesture that might have been intended as comforting, but left her with the irritated feeling that he'd made a pass at her. 'Just let me say one more time, it's a great pleasure to see you again.'

Kyla felt her nostrils dilate with distaste as his dark brown gaze slithered over her body.

'Thanks, Alex. I'll see you, then.'

As he turned away, relief surged through her. Her gaze followed him as he went out into the hallway and made for the front door, her breath hissed out thankfully when she heard it slam shut.

Lord, but she needed a drink herself after that! She knew that Alexander Gordon did all the legal work for Ferguson Whisky. She also knew that she couldn't work with the man—regardless of the fact that as a lawyer he was second to none in the county—unless she let him know from day one that as a woman she was unavailable, and unavailable with a capital U!

That was something she'd have to think about before Monday, but not now. . .

As she made for the well-stocked buffet-table by the door, for the hundredth time since she came downstairs she gave in to the overpowering compulsion to search the crowded room for a sight of Adam. Excusing herself as she bumped into someone she'd talked to earlier, she scanned the many groups of people, looking for the finely shaped dark head and broad shoulders she so dreaded seeing.

He wasn't there. Her heart began to thud as if someone were banging against it with a giant gong. Her fingers shook as she reached for the decanter, and she knew that if she didn't stop thinking about Adam she was going to make herself ill.

She leaned her hip against the table and, gulping down a large mouthful of sherry so quickly that the strong, fiery liquid almost made her choke, she tried to shut out her torment by concentrating on the familiar surroundings.

She had always loved the drawing-room at Glencraig House, and it hadn't changed much over the past five years. Perhaps the walls had been painted, she reflected distractedly, and perhaps the red carpet with its pattern of silver whorls looked slightly worn in front of the fireplace. But the elegant Ercol furniture, the floral Sanderson curtains, the red velvet cushions arranged casually on the comfortable armchairs and sofas, looked just as they had on her last visit.

It was a pleasant room in summer, and on a bleak, dark afternoon like this, with an occasional threatening gust of wind rattling the huge window-panes, it was cosy despite its great size. A coal fire was blazing cheerily in the brass-trimmed hearth, its arc of warmth supplemented by the white-painted radiators placed strategically at the windows.

'I'd like to say how sorry I was to hear about your father-in-law's death. . .'

Kyla started, spilling a few drops of sherry. She hadn't noticed the approach of the heavy-set woman whose speckled blue eyes were now examining her from behind thick-lensed spectacles.

'Oh, Mrs Webster, how nice to see you.' Kyla transferred her glass to her left hand and with a smile accepted the stubby fingers extended to her, the red-veined cheek offered in greeting. 'It was awfully good of you to turn out on such a wintry afternoon.'

As she chatted with Glencraig's retired postmistress, Kyla's thoughts strayed involuntarily once again to Adam. Where had he gone after he'd come into the house? Was it possible that he was as eager as she was to postpone their first meeting? Had he already shown his face at the reception and then left, perhaps when she had been deep in conversation with someone, or perhaps while she had dawdled upstairs, combing her hair, touching up her make-up, smoothing her black dress over her too-thin hips?

'I hear you and Drew had a son. He's here with you?' Eyes that glittered with curiosity peered through the thick lenses. 'He'd be. . .what, now—four?'

A wry grin curved Kyla's lips. She hadn't forgotten that everyone in Glencraig knew everyone else's business, and that the most reliable source of knowledge had always been Fanny Webster.

'Yes, four, Mrs Webster,' she answered patiently. 'And yes, he's here with me. It's wonderful to be back. I can't tell you how I've missed the town, and the folk.'

While they were talking, several others had gathered round and were listening to the conversation, glasses in one hand, fruitcake in the other.

'You'll know everybody here, then? You remember the Whites from Abermore?' Fanny pointed with one ringed index finger to an elderly couple who had just moved to the fringe of their group. She was obviously enjoying being in the limelight. 'And of course,' her voice shrilled excitedly as her eyes swivelled over Kyla's left shoulder and rose to a point a good foot above it, 'you know *this* handsome young man!'

Without looking round, Kyla knew that it was Adam. He was so close that she could feel his breath ruffle the long strands of hair that hung at her shoulders.

In the time since she'd come downstairs, the buzz of sound in the room had been growing louder and louder in direct proportion to the amount of whisky and sherry consumed. Now she felt as if she were in the tower of Babel, and her head was filled with a confusion of voices.

'Handsome? Fanny Webster, as I've told you many a time, you could charm the birds out of the trees with your flattery! And thirty-five may seem young to you, but I'm sure that to the likes of Mrs Ferguson here, who is still in her twenties, it must seem quite ancient.'

Kyla jumped nervously as her elbow was cupped in a rough grip, and her heart lurched at Adam's low, husky chuckle. 'Now, if you'll excuse us, Fanny, I have some matters to discuss with our visitor from Canada.'

Beads of perspiration coated Kyla's upper lip. For a wild, senseless moment, she wished that she hadn't lost so much weight during the past year, wished that the black dress didn't drain her complexion of its last vestiges of colour, wished that the lines of strain could be erased from her face.

And then her wishes scattered, for she had to concentrate all her attention on just keeping her legs from buckling under her. Her feet stumbled several times as Adam steered her across the room, and when he twisted her round so that her back was pressed against the curtained window, she was thankful that his tall frame hid her ashen features from the others in the room.

'So, you did come back.'

The sound of his voice conjured up memories that Kyla had carefully secreted away years before; now they began to escape, setting her heart into a wild frenzy. No amount of will-power could steady the hand that she reached out, no amount of praying could erase the tremor from her voice as she murmured, 'Adam.'

She raised her head and looked straight up into his face.

Not fair, her heart screamed out, not fair; I should have had some warning. The sharp edges of her teeth bit into her lips as she stifled the impulse to cry out. Oh, lord, did *I* do this to him?

The last time she'd seen him, his hair had been short and well-cut, and black as a midnight forest. Now it was silvered, as if by the fingers of a midnight moon, and it was too long, falling carelessly over his forehead, and curling over the white collar of his shirt. His eyes too had changed. Kyla remembered them as being the grey of ancient pewter, with pewter's soft, rich gleam; now they were hard, hostile, guarded—as impenetrable as Aberdeen granite. Even his features looked as if they had been carved from rock; lines were etched on his wide brow, and even more deeply engraved down his cheeks from his proud, straight nose to his sardonically curved mouth. His features were set in a grim, forbidding mould, as if it were a very, very long time since he'd found anything to smile about.

A strong hand clasped hers, grinding the large sapphire ring on her finger against the bone so that she winced. 'My condolences. . .' he paused almost imperceptibly before going on '. . .Mrs Ferguson.' The way he said her name turned it into an insult. 'Your father-in-law will be missed around these parts.' He dropped her hand, and deliberately wiped his own against the fine English worsted sheathing his thigh. 'And now. . .you've come to collect.'

The muscles at Kyla's nape ached as she looked up at him. 'What? I don't quite——'

'I said,' he repeated with an insolent curl of his lip, 'you've come to collect.'

'Explain yourself.' Kyla stood her ground as his gaze ran scornfully over the jewels at her ears and the silk scarf at her throat. Her eyelids barely flickered as he stared at the gold brooch on her lapel.

'I don't think I have to spell it out, do I? You've got it all now, haven't you? The furs, the diamonds, the easy life. All the things you so desired, all the things you believed you couldn't expect to get from me.'

Kyla thought the stem of her glass might snap as her fingers tightened round it. 'I had hoped that we could all put the past behind us and——'

'Ah!' She froze as he leaned closer, one broad shoulder trapping her between him and the window. 'Ah, so *that's* what you want. To have your cake and eat it too. Well, Mrs Ferguson, someone should have told you before you came all this way that that's not possible.'

'Don't talk to me in that superior tone, Adam. As far as I'm concerned, the past is the past. If you want to keep raking it up, then go and join some of those old biddies——' she half turned towards a trio of women who were huddled together on a sofa '——and get down to their level.' She moved to sidestep him, but he swiftly forestalled her, grabbing one of her small hands in his and twisting her arm so that she cried out softly.

Despite the stab of pain, Kyla was intensely aware of the effect the touch of his callused palm was having on her.

Incredibly powerful currents of. . .*something*. . .were surging up her arm, tingling their way to every single sensitive part of her body, parts which she'd believed to be dead. . .

Adam's smooth drawl interrupted her dangerous train of thought. 'But tell me, how long do you intend to stay? A week? Ten days? You'll be missing the city lights already, I imagine.'

Kyla felt dizzy with the emotions churning around inside her, but she knew that as long as she was in Adam's presence she hadn't a hope in the world of sorting them out. 'City lights?' A tight smile twisted her lips as she shook her head. 'No, Adam, I don't miss Toronto. I guess what they say is true—you can take the girl out of the country, but you can't take the country out of the girl. I've missed Glencraig. This is my home, and this is where I want to be.' She tilted her chin determinedly as she stared up at him. 'This is where I intend to bring up my son.'

She could see that her reply had taken Adam completely by surprise. For a moment all his contempt and hostility dropped away, and for that moment the old Adam was back. Open, vulnerable. . .and startled. Then in a flash his eyes were again as blank as shuttered windows.

'You're planning to take up residence here, at Glencraig House?' Though his words were softly spoken, they held a definite, steely challenge.

Kyla was suddenly conscious that the heat from the radiator was uncomfortable against her silk-sheathed legs. She slid past Adam, standing so her back was to the room.

'That's right.'

Now that she was a couple of feet away from him, he seemed even more magnificent than he'd been five years ago. She had never seen him in a dark suit before. Always on the farm he'd worn ancient cords and warm

Viyella shirts; when they'd met in the evenings, he'd changed to well-pressed jeans, and a heather-toned Harris tweed jacket with leather patches on the elbows. Now he looked very formal, with his spotless white shirt, and the black tie—the token of his mourning.

With a rapidity that shook her, all the fight drained out of Kyla. 'Look, Adam, I'm tired. I drove up here from Prestwick yesterday, and didn't get much sleep last night. It's been a trying day. If you've got anything more to say, get it off your chest and leave me alone.'

'You're thinner.'

The abruptness of his response took her breath away.

'So?' Her whisper was like the rustle of dry leaves.

'And you look older. Older than you should.'

Kyla knew only too well that he was speaking the truth, yet it still hurt to hear him say it. 'Anything else?'

She watched Adam run his fingers inside his shirt collar. 'Just one more thing. . .for now. Why didn't you answer your mother's letters? She did write to you, didn't she, after she heard that you and Drew had had a son?'

Kyla's eyes slid away from his as she made a pretence of looking for somewhere to lay her empty glass. 'After what happened,' she said, her fingers shaking as she leaned over to a round table by the window, 'I thought it better to make a clean break.'

There was a pause, as Adam stared down at her, his expression inscrutable. 'After what happened. . .' Why had she said that? She hadn't meant ever to refer to the past. What was he going to say? Would he use her remark as a stepping-stone to tread into the dark shadows that lay between them?

'But you're going to see her now. . .and your father, and Nairne? You'll have to, won't you, if you're going to settle here?' A look of genuine puzzlement flitted across his features. 'I must admit I'm curious as hell to find out why Glencraig is all of a sudden the chosen place. . .'

Kyla breathed a silent prayer of thanks that he wasn't—for now, at any rate—going to take her for a walk into the past. 'Yes, I'm going to see them. And there's no secret about my reasons for wanting to return to Glencraig.' She gestured helplessly with her hands. 'It's for Kevin's sake. He needs a family. He. . .he's becoming ill. He misses Drew so. . .' Kyla felt her throat tighten. Kevin wasn't the only one to miss Drew. Tears pricked at the back of her eyes. She missed him so much, too.

Adam's speculative gaze narrowed, and a look of—was it compassion? Surely not!—flashed between them for a fraction of a second, and then it was gone. She saw him nod, his jaw muscles tighten, as if he understood. Understood, but misunderstood. She missed Drew, but not in the way she'd missed Adam when she'd run away from him and his love.

Then he was reaching out to her, and afterwards she wondered if he'd really touched her, his gesture had been so fleeting. She thought the pad of his thumb had brushed the soft, red curve of her mouth, trailing in a tender path along the sensitive flesh. . .

'You've still got your bee-stung lip.'

Kyla was glad that her skin was a pale ivory that never blushed. She remembered only too well the first time that he had used that phrase to describe her sensual lower lip. They had been making love in the heather, on a fine June afternoon, at the head of Loch Craig. She remembered the warmth of the rug against her naked back, remembered how she'd heard a skylark warbling in the cloudless sky as he brushed his lips over the thrusting tip of her breast. . .

'And you've still got your forward manners,' she retorted unevenly, grateful that she could speak at all as she pushed his hand away and thanked heaven that he couldn't possibly see the quivering effect his closeness was having on every responsive nerve-ending in her body. 'Nothing changes, does it?'

Their eyes met, and Kyla felt as if she were looking directly into the sun. Dear heaven, she thought, as the realisation struck her like a bolt of lightning, dear heaven, it was true. Nothing *had* changed. Not for her, anyway. She was still in love with Adam Garvie. She was *blinded* by her love for him, and the heat of it flared through her, fanning the long-banked embers into a terrifying blaze.

All the background sounds faded away. She could no longer hear the noisy buzz of conversation, or the spark and hiss of the fire. All she was aware of was his harsh breathing. . .or was it her own?

'*Damn!*' she heard him mutter savagely. 'Why in hell's name did you have to come back?'

With a speed that caught her completely unprepared, he gripped her upper arms, crushing them as if they were twigs he wanted to snap in two. Kyla's lips parted on an indrawn protesting gasp as his breath, intimate and, even after five years, excitingly familiar, burned hot against her cheeks, and the tantalisingly male scent of his body assaulted her senses.

And then, just when she thought she'd cry out with pain, and her aching need for him, he flung her away. Before she had time to steady herself or even catch her breath, he brushed past, issuing one last verbal slap before he strode across the room and out through the open doorway.

She closed her eyes against the invective. It hurt more than she would ever want him to know that his opinion of her was so low.

But regardless of the fact that he didn't know the truth, and never would, she still found it heart-breaking that, given the love they had once shared, the promises they had once made, he hadn't trusted her enough five years ago to realise that she must have had some very good reasons for acting the way she had.

And over and over again in the darkness behind her eyelids, spinning and whirling like the rising wind outside, his cruel, parting taunt spiralled around in her head.

'Gold-digging *bitch*!'

CHAPTER TWO

'SUGAR? On his *porridge*? I'm sure you would have considered that sacrilege when Drew was a boy!'

Kyla's anxious face relaxed a little as she watched Martha sprinkle some demerara sugar on to Kevin's warm cereal, then quickly tensed again as her son murmured a quiet 'thank you' but made no attempt to touch the spoon set out on the yellow and white chequered tablecloth in front of him.

'Aren't you hungry, Kev?'

The rhythmic chugging of the washing-machine in the laundry alcove by the door seemed to resound in Kyla's head as she looked over the top of the pottery milk jug at the small figure sitting across from her. His chin was buried in the loose neckline of his turquoise wool sweater, and all she could see was the slow shaking of his head, the reddish-fair hair gleaming under the kitchen's fluorescent lights.

The fragrant smell of the bacon she and Martha had breakfasted on still hung in the air, mingling with the delicious aroma from a spicy dish simmering in the oven for lunch. Kyla glanced at the gold-framed wall clock. It was nearly ten o'clock, she realised, yet it was still almost dark outside.

In the small hours of the morning, the fierce storm she had anticipated had come sweeping down from the Arctic. When the gale-force winds had set the window-panes shuddering, she had been lying awake in her big bed, unable to stop thinking about her confrontation with Adam. After what had happened five years ago, Adam Garvie had been the last person she would have expected to attend the funeral of a Ferguson.

24

Perhaps he and Barclay had done business together, she'd reflected as she'd pulled the duvet up to her chin; perhaps he had sold his barley crop each year to Ferguson Whisky. At any rate, she'd decided, frowning as the storm had rattled the slates on the roof and whistled round the chimney-pots, there would be no reason in the future for him to visit Glencraig House. Any business transactions with Ferguson Whisky could be carried out with whomever she hired to manage the estate.

Had he thought that he could frighten her away with his hurtful accusations? She'd wiped away the suspicion of a tear with the hem of one crisp lavender-scented sheet. No, he could never do that. She was going to stay in Glencraig, no matter what. Kevin's well-being was more important than anything in the world to her. . .more important even than the pain in her heart because of Adam's cruelty.

The last sound in her ears as she had finally fallen asleep had been once again his angry, contemptuous voice. . .'Gold-digging *bitch*. . .'

She jumped as Martha unwittingly brought her back to the present by dropping a pan lid on the floor. Blinking, she shook her head. . .and felt more wretched than ever when she saw that Kevin was still staring down at his untouched plate.

'Sweetheart?' She reached across the table and dipped the tip of his spoon into the sweetened porridge and cream. 'Won't you just taste it?'

'OK, Mom.'

With an apathy that tore at her heart, he raised his head a little and, taking the spoon from her, slid the porridge into his mouth. Then he continued eating, chewing and swallowing as mechanically as if he were a robot.

Kyla pushed back her chair and walked to the sink where Martha had her hands plunged into hot, soapy water.

'I wonder if I should take him to see some kind of a specialist?' She spoke softly so that Kevin wouldn't hear. 'Perhaps he should be having grief therapy. . .' She absently lifted a dish-towel and began drying the break-fast dishes as the housekeeper, slotted them into the plastic rack.

Martha's derisive snort startled her. 'Grief therapy!' The movement of her hands halted as she turned to face Kyla. 'And what good would that do, missy?'

'Don't scoff.' Kyla stared out at the huge copper beech trees that flanked the driveway leading to the back door. Their winter-bare branches were being twisted by the savage gusts of wind snarling over the fields. 'Experts say that there are different stages of grief, and that people can be helped through them——'

'I know what the experts say.' Martha pulled out the plug and let the soapy water drain away. Drying her hands, she reached into the pocket of her apron and drew out a packet of Craven A and a box of Swan Vestas matches. Extricating a king-size filtertip, she placed it carelessly between her lips. 'Glencraig may be a back-water, missy,' she said out of the corner of her mouth as she stuffed the pack back into her pocket, 'but we do get newspapers here. I know what's going on in the world.'

With an exaggerated gesture, she struck a match.

Before she could carry the orange flame to her ciga-rette, Kyla interjected swiftly, 'If you know so much about what's going on, Martha, then you must be well aware of the dangers of second-hand smoke. . .' She let her words trail away as she gestured significantly towards Kevin.

There was a pause as long green eyes met wide hazel ones in candid challenge, the air between strong with the smell of sulphur. Then, just as the match burned to within a hair's breadth of Martha's finger and thumb, she blew it out.

'Thanks, Martha. I appreciate it.'

Kyla breathed a silent sigh of relief as Martha tossed the discarded cigarette on to the windowsill. During the many years when she had come to Glencraig House as a child, Martha had ruled the household, and Kyla had always treated her with respect. Now the situation was reversed, and the best course was to start as she meant to go on. She was mistress of the house, and Martha was her servant. She had never had a servant before, but surely if she just behaved naturally, and spoke her mind, they'd get along as well as they always had? It seemed that the elderly housekeeper was prepared to meet her half-way.

'You'll be taking the bairn over to Tigh Na Mara today to meet his grandparents, and his auntie?' Martha shuffled from the sink to the fridge, her steps muffled in her beige carpet slippers. She took out a bag of carrots and dumped it on the countertop. 'They were to get back from their European bus tour late last night.'

Despite the housekeeper's offhand tone, Kyla knew she wasn't as casual as she sounded. She draped the damp dish-towel over the plastic rack, hoping that her own expression hadn't given away her feelings of apprehension. She had already confronted Adam, and he had spurned her attempts to put the past behind them. What if she met with the same reaction at Tigh Na Mara? What if Nairne too was still so bitter that she couldn't allow herself to forgive her elder sister?

Kyla opened one of the cupboards and began putting away the dishes, the china rattling beneath her trembling fingers. 'Yes, we'll drive over there in the afternoon and visit for a little while, won't we, Kevin? Now, drink up your milk and then we'll go for that walk I promised you, down to the distillery.'

'You're going down to the still? Just around the dam, or were you planning on taking him inside?'

The steady rhythm of knife scraping against carrot

hesitated, and a subtle tension seemed to seep into the atmosphere. Kyla frowned uneasily.

'Not inside, Martha. Not today. We'll do things nice and easy.' She threw a questioning glance at the housekeeper, but she was once again concentrating on the task at hand. I'm imagining things, Kyla decided—and surely I've enough problems already without creating more myself!

She swivelled round with an attempt at gaiety, holding out her arms to Kevin.

'Come over here, sweetheart,' she coaxed.

The four-year-old walked listlessly round the long table, and Kyla had to bite back an emotional exclamation as she swung his slight body up on to the edge of the sink. 'Look, from this window you can see some of the places where your Daddy used to play when he was your age.'

She examined his thin little face as he turned to look outside. His features were almost a miniature of his father's, with Drew's straight, well-formed nose, sleek, reddish-fair eyebrows, and high, nicely rounded cheekbones. Not a handsome face, but attractive and appealing. His eyes, at present staring gravely along the driveway, were hazel, like her own. Large, fringed with dark lashes, they made his face look small and plaintive.

Kyla's eyelids closed briefly as she dropped a kiss on top of his head.

'A car's coming.' Kevin's sweet breath tickled her nostrils. 'It's a man.'

With eager, stained fingers, Martha twitched back the edge of the yellow and white gingham curtains.

'The laddie's right.' Short yellowed curls bobbed in affirmation. 'Someone *is* coming.' Her statement was followed by a delighted, expectant chuckle. 'And och aye, there's no denying the fact that our visitor's a *man*!'

Kyla felt her hands tighten round Kevin's waist as she looked out of the window.

Oh, no, she thought, her swift, involuntary surge of joy swept away by a wave of panic, I've got to get out of here.

A large black car was parked at the end of the drive, and Adam was walking briskly up the path to the back door, his bare head bent against the bitter wind. Dressed in a sheepskin coat that was being whipped away from his lean body by the gale, and well-pressed jeans that seemed to be bonded to his legs, revealing and emphasising their length and power, he was *all* man. Kyla's heartbeats tripped frantically over each other, with the speed of bullets ripping from a machine gun. Her mind, on the other hand, had slowed to a complete standstill; it wasn't capable of one sensible thought.

She dropped Kevin to the floor. 'Let's run upstairs.' Her voice had the strength of a gnat's. 'We'll get our warm things on and——'

'Running never solved anything.' Martha fixed Kyla with eyes that were suddenly shining like green glass beads. 'You should have found that out by——'

Whatever she had been going to say was cut off by the sound of the back door slamming. Seconds later, the kitchen door burst open and, just like a blast of wind from the Arctic, Adam swept into the room, bringing with him the clean smell of the outdoors.

Kyla bit her lip to hide its trembling. It was too late. She was trapped.

Kevin's head was pressed against her leg, and she let her hands fall on to his shoulders, whether to reassure him or herself she couldn't tell. She wanted to turn and run, despite Martha's warning words, for she knew from bitter experience that running was the only solution to some problems. . .

It was almost unbearable to be in the same room as Adam. His deep baritone 'good morning' tugged at her heartstrings as he shrugged off his sheepskin coat and hung it on a hook behind the door.

How unutterably drab and uninteresting she felt in her grey skirt and black cowl-neck when she saw the beautiful red V-necked sweater he was wearing over an icy blue shirt. The contrast with his ebony, silvered hair was stunning; his presence, vibrantly, compellingly masculine, seemed to reach out to her across the kitchen.

In the brief moment when he had his back to her, Kyla's glance stole reluctantly over his broad shoulders, moving over their rugged outline before sliding down the tapered shape to his lean waist.

Then, to her everlasting shame, her gaze glided even further, drawn irresistibly to the taut curve of his buttocks under the denim of his jeans, the steely muscles of his legs that told of hours spent hiking along the local moors, and challenging the dangerous rock walls of Mount Craigie.

The pain in Kyla's heart was exquisite. She couldn't look at him without remembering what he had looked like naked, and how, the first time they had made love, it had surprised her that a man's shoulders and arms could be so tough and corded, his chest so matted with springy, black hair, yet the skin in other places, under the tentative, inexperienced touch of her fingertips, so satin-smooth, so sweetly exciting——

She blinked as she realised that they were all looking at her. Martha's round face was cocked to one side, her hands in her apron pockets; Kevin had his arms round her leg, his brow wrinkled in a frown; and Adam. . .Adam was staring at her, his grey eyes narrowed.

She felt the blood drain from her face. Had they all seen her caressing his body with her eyes?

'I'm sorry. . .did. . .did someone say something?'

'Martha suggested she make some coffee.' Adam's voice was curt. He brushed back his wind-tossed hair impatiently from his forehead as he reached into the cupboard and drew out a yellow canister. 'And I said that sounded like a good idea.'

He took the jug from the coffee-maker and filled it almost to the top with cold water. Kyla's eyes widened in surprise. It was obviously not the first time Adam Garvie had had elevenses here.

'Come on, Martha, get the mugs out.' Tweaking the elderly woman's apron-strings, he slid the coffee-pot into place.

Kyla's heartbeats had been galloping behind her breastbone ever since she had seen Adam coming up the path to the back door, and now, as he turned to her, she felt them break loose, like the thundering hooves of a runaway horse. The memory of the insult he'd flung at her last night still tore at her. Had he forgotten? Or was he going to act as if nothing had happened between them?

And, if so, would he really expect that she could do the same? He had accused her of marrying Drew for the Ferguson money. Maybe it was irrational of her, but she couldn't forgive him for that.

Adam's cool voice disturbed her thoughts. 'I trust you slept well?' She pressed her lips together, knowing he didn't expect an answer, as he stared at her as dispassionately as if she were a mannequin in a store window. He started at her hair, which hung loosely around her shoulders, then moved down her thin figure, examining her breasts, her hips, and her long, silk-stockinged legs.

With a sigh which Kyla didn't know signified weariness or just plain boredom, he turned away from her and, thrusting his hands into his jeans pockets, appeared to notice Kevin for the first time.

Kyla felt a quiver of expectation as she observed him from under her long lashes, well aware that the tension that already existed in the room had suddenly tightened to breaking point.

Kevin had slid away from Kyla's side, and was

standing with his back to the table, eyes fixed on Adam. Kyla's heart clenched. When Adam looked at him, he would see only Drew. Would he be as hostile to Drew's son as he was to Drew's widow?

The coffee-maker gurgled into the savoury kitchen air, a pleasant accompaniment to the even, whirring sound of the washing-machine which was now in the spin cycle. . .and to Martha's surprisingly musical humming. Kyla had no difficulty recognising the tune she'd chosen: 'Stormy Weather'. If she hadn't been so distressed, she'd have laughed aloud. The old biddy still had all her faculties about her, there was no doubt about that. Any minute now she'd be breaking into 'The Way We Were'!

Adam scrutinised Kevin's small features with an intensity that sent a shiver of anxiety through Kyla. His lips were compressed, a muscle quivered under his left cheekbone.

Then Kyla relaxed as, for the first time since coming back to Glencraig, she saw Adam's face light up in a genuine, warm smile.

'Seems we're going to have to introduce ourselves, young man. I'm Adam Garvie from Redhillock Farm, just down the glen from here. And you must be Kevin.' Adam crouched down on his haunches and took one small hand in his, shaking it briefly. 'I've been looking forward to meeting you. . .' He gently pushed back the fringe wisping over Kevin's brow, and said softly, 'You're very like your father. You must be pleased about that.'

Kyla couldn't have spoken if her life had depended on it. Tears welled up in her eyes, and she had to look away. Dear lord, Adam was incredible. One minute his insensitive attitude was flinging her into a white-hot rage, the next he was saying all the right things to Kevin and her heart was filled to overflowing with love and gratitude. She bit her lip hard in an effort to regain control of herself.

Kevin's eyes slid away shyly, and moved to the table, where Martha had set out three mugs, along with a pottery sugar bowl and cream jug. Kyla watched, tears still in her eyes, as his dark-fringed hazel gaze turned back to Adam, an almost imperceptible frown knitting his pale forehead. Adam glanced quickly round, and his grey eyes sparked.

'Three? Aren't you forgetting someone, Martha?'

Martha didn't look up as she arranged some tea biscuits on a flowered plate. 'No, that I'm not. The laddie's far too young to drink coffee. He'll get another glass of milk.'

Kyla could see Kevin's shoulder tense. When Drew had been alive, he'd often told him teasingly, 'When you're a man, you'll be able to drink coffee,' and Kevin had grinned up at him, as if it were a private joke.

Now Adam sprang up again, but not before Kyla saw the conspiratorial wink he threw in Kevin's direction.

'Nonsense. He's the man of the family now. He can have a cup of coffee with the adults now and again. Won't do him any harm.'

Martha snorted, and looked at Kyla for guidance. Kyla turned away to hide her watery smile.

Why was it so painful to see Adam and Kevin together? Was it because, if things had been different five years ago, this could have Adam's own son, Adam's and hers?

'Just this once, Martha.' Kyla avoided looking at Adam as she sat down, pulling Kevin on to a chair beside her. 'It won't do him any harm if we don't make a habit of it.'

She couldn't help wondering if Adam was as upset to find her here as she was to find him. It seemed not. He was smiling casually as he strolled across to the coffee-maker.

'Sit down, Martha,' he drawled, taking the pot from her thin, gnarled fingers. 'I'll do that.'

Kyla played nervously with the corner of the gingham tablecloth as he filled the mugs. When he came to the fourth, he filled it three-quarters full with milk, added some sugar, and then splashed a mere tablespoonful of the scalding brown liquid on top.

'There, Kevin. That'll put hair on your chest.'

Kyla bit her lip as she watched Kevin sip his coffee. Drew had had a distinctive way of holding his mug, an unusual way of curling his fingers round the handle, and Kevin had managed to mimic his father's grip exactly. He was watching Adam over the rim of the mug, sizing up this stranger who was giving out orders in the house his mother had told him was their new home. It was quite obvious that he was puzzled.

Martha hummed the last few bars of 'Stormy Weather' as, coffee-mug in hand, she made for the door.

'Where are you off to, Martha?' Adam pulled out a chair and sprawled on to it lazily. 'Aren't we good enough for you today?'

'Going through to my room.' As the door swung shut behind her, Kyla heard the mumbled, 'Second-hand smoke!' and she felt her lips tremble in a smile.

'What do you think of Glencraig, Kevin?'

Kevin looked up at Adam, his eyes wary. 'I don't know yet.' His pale cheeks coloured slightly as he subjected Adam to a scrutiny as close as the one to which he himself had been subjected a short while before. 'I'm finished, Mom,' he said, still looking at the man sitting across the table from him. 'May I go upstairs and get my jacket?'

It was obvious that this large, good-looking stranger intrigued Kevin. Like mother, like son, thought Kyla wryly, as she drained her coffee in one long swallow, hardly tasting the strong, aromatic brew. 'Yes, of course, honey. I'll come with you. Will you excuse us?' Her

chair grated on the kitchen floor as she pushed back
from the table, and she caught Kevin as he slid to the
floor. 'We've made some plans for the morning.' She
held the little body against her like a shield and faced
Adam defiantly. 'I promised we'd go for a walk round
the distillery buildings so Kevin can get the lie of the
land.'

She watched, her heart in her throat as Adam drained
his mug and stood up. He towered over her, his grey
eyes impaling her.

'Then I could have saved myself the journey here this
morning. There's a couple of things I want to discuss
with you. Drop by the office as you're passing.'

Kyla felt her fingers tighten on Kevin's shoulders as
Adam walked to the door.

'Office?' It annoyed her that she sounded so vacant,
but she hadn't a clue what he was talking about. 'What
office?'

'The office at the distillery.' He thrust his arms into
the sheepskin jacket and shrugged it on. 'I thought you
knew. Barclay had been ill for some time. He wasn't able
to manage the business any longer.'

The smile on his face as he stopped by the door was
no longer casual and relaxed; it was hard and contemptuous. Kyla felt Kevin wince under her rough grasp.
Heavens, but Adam Garvie was arrogant and overbear-
ing. What was his exit line going to be this time?

She didn't have long to wait for her answer. . .and,
when it came, she realised why Martha had seemed so
tense when Kyla had mentioned going down to the
distillery.

'Barclay hired me as manager. In addition to farming
Redhillock, I've been working for Ferguson Whisky. I
have a five-year contract that's water-tight. You and I,
my dear Kyla, shall be working together.'

Kyla struggled to assimilate the information he'd flung
at her. 'Working together'. The words echoed in her

head, swirling round and round till she felt dizzy. Then the sensation cleared and miraculously she knew what she had to do. Just as she had with Martha, she had to establish right away who was boss. Start as she meant to go on.

'This is a surprise,' she said steadily. 'I didn't keep in touch with Barclay after Drew died. . .'

She saw Adam's dark eyebrows rise; she knew they would rise even further if she told him the real reason why she had not wanted to talk or write to the old man. 'I. . .I've been so concerned with Kevin. . .' Briefly she glanced at Kevin, and knew she wasn't actually telling a lie. She had been worried sick about him. 'I had no idea Barclay was so ill.' She gripped the back of the chair in front of her, trying to control the shaking that always seemed to start whenever she thought of the past, of what Barclay had done. . .

Her voice was almost steady as she went on, 'And, as you now know, I had no idea you were managing the distillery. So,' she flexed her fingers tautly, 'for the moment, till I've had time to go over everything with Alex Gordon—and we've already set up an appointment for Monday—you and I *shall*, as you say, be working together.'

Adam opened his mouth to speak, but before he had time to say anything Kyla proceeded smoothly, 'However, as to seeing you in your office today, I'm afraid that's out of the question. I plan on devoting the morning to Kevin, and then in the afternoon, I. . .' She cleared her throat of the huskiness that had rasped in it at the thought of seeing her parents and Nairne again. 'This afternoon, we're going to Tigh Na Mara; Martha tells me my folks were away on holiday, and were to have returned last night. So I'm afraid our talk will have to wait. After I've spoken to Alex, I'll give you a call.'

A comical, startled expression flitted across Adam's

lean, weather-beaten face. It was so fleeting that afterwards Kyla had to wonder if it had been there at all, or
if she had misinterpreted it. Then, with eyes dark as a
winter's night over Loch Craig, he wheeled away, his
heavy brogues making the floor tremble as he crashed
out of the room.

Kyla wondered if Adam had ever had a woman dish
out orders to him before. Probably not. With his dark,
rakish looks and his disarming smile, he probably had
every woman in the county of Moray burning to carry
out *his* orders! She bit her lip to curtail a hysterical laugh
as she imagined women lining up in their hundreds,
eagerly waiting to do his bidding. . .

The back door thundered shut with such a reverber-
ating crack that the noise must have echoed right through
the large house. Out of nowhere Martha suddenly shuffled into the kitchen, a long cigarette dangling precariously from her lower lip. 'What the devil——'

'Adam.' Kyla's near hysteria had evaporated before it
had really started. She shivered, as if someone had just
walked over her grave, and her fingers were white as
they gripped the back of the chair. 'He just left.'

'Ah.' Martha exhaled, and through the cloud of grey
smoke circling her cocked head Kyla could see a smug
green glitter. 'Then the wind must have caught the
door.'

She glanced first at Kevin, then at her cigarette, before
shuffling with a loud 'Humph!' over to the sink where
she ran a stream of cold water over the glowing tip.

'That storm I mentioned yesterday. . .I saw it coming,
missy. I warned you.' Her laugh was a grim cackle in the
still kitchen. 'It's here. . .with a vengeance.'

CHAPTER THREE

THE silver Bentley was a dream to drive, but Kyla's knuckles were white on the red steering wheel as she struggled to manoeuvre it safely down Milton Hill from Glencraig House that afternoon. The gale that was spinning the grey clouds across the stormy skies and whistling over the bare, ploughed fields, also tugged at the powerful vehicle, making it difficult for her to keep it on the narrow road.

She switched on the radio to shut out the wild moaning outside, and as the soundtrack of *La Bamba* filled the car she rounded a corner and caught a fleeting glimpse of Glencraig down below, its street-lights already twinkling in the near darkness.

The little town was situated along a stretch of the mile-long Loch Craig, its high street hugging the shore as if to protect it from inclement weather. But as Kyla swung on to the bramble-lined road curling along the lochside, she reflected that even if the bungalows and two-storey houses had been as tall as Toronto's CN Tower they would have been an ineffective shield from the storm howling in today from the North Sea.

The gunmetal-grey waters were whipped into a seething, foaming cauldron, with waves surging up angrily in a futile attempt to catch the gusting intruder as it drove them mercilessly from one shore to the other. The delicate stems of the reeds at the water's edge had bowed to the ground before the marauding wind, and even the fir trees, despite their sturdy trunks, had bent in awkward, reluctant homage.

Humming absently along with the throbbing male voice on the radio, Kyla glanced at Kevin, cocooned in his navy snowsuit, a case of Lego in his lap. He had shown little interest during their morning walk around the distillery buildings, but when they had run down the path to the dam he had thrown a few stones into the storm-driven water. The damp chill of the wind had penetrated Kyla's jacket, so they hadn't stayed long, but it had been a pleasure to see some colour in Kevin's pale cheeks when they'd arrived back in Martha's kitchen for a delicious lunch of shepherd's pie.

A ripple of excitement thrilled through her as they rounded the last corner, and her old home—the first house at this end of town—suddenly came into view. When she saw the small granite villa nestled like a haven in its arc of birch trees, lights on in a couple of the windows, she forgot for a moment the dread that had been twisting her stomach ever since lunchtime.

'There it is, Kevin,' she said, her voice tight with suppressed excitement. 'Tigh Na Mara.'

She slowed the car, whether to savour the moment or to delay their arrival, she wasn't quite sure. Kevin was straining to peek out of the window, and wryly she realised that while all he saw was a red-roofed house, with a bay window looking out on to the loch, and a chimney with white smoke streaming in the wind, for her the unpretentious building represented a large part of her life.

'Did you live here with Grandma?'

Wet, black leaves slapped against the windscreen, and Kyla frowned as she hunted on the unfamiliar dashboard for the wiper switch.

'Five years ago. . .' She grimaced as the wiper arm squashed the leaves down into the moulding.

Had it really been just five years since she had left? Five years since that day when she'd discovered that Kathleen O'Malley Drummond—devoted wife, caring mother, and talented artist, a woman blessed with all the

charm and beauty of the Emerald Isle itself—was not
what she seemed?

Tension began knotting inside her again as she drove
on to the shoulder and parked alongside the cotoneaster
hedge.

'Now,' she said, unbuckling Kevin's belt with
unsteady fingers, 'they don't know we're coming, so let's
go give them a big surprise!'

The wind almost blew them off their feet as they ran
along the crazy paving that ran from the rickety green
gate to the front door, and Kyla's long black hair was
tangled across her face so she could hardly see as she
reached for the bell.

She held the strands back from her chilled cheeks as
her eyes greedily drank in all the familiar things around
her: the green and red gnome sitting on the top step, the
ivy creeping up the wall, the forsythia bush which had
flourished by the bay window for as long as she could
remember.

Her stomach started to cramp with nerves, and she
bent over, clutching herself. She closed her eyes, trying
to fight back the feeling that she was going to be sick.
Oh, please, let there be nobody home.

But that would just be delaying the inevitable; she *had*
to go through with it. For Kevin's sake.

She raised a weak fist to knock on the door, and as she
did she heard someone coming. The floor of the hallway
at Tigh Na Mara had always been uncarpeted, its ancient
oak planking worn smooth with the passage of time and
many feet. Now Kyla could hear a light, jaunty step
cross it, and someone calling out, 'I'll get it, Mac.'

Kyla straightened hurriedly, swallowing back her
anxious gasp. There was no mistaking that Irish voice
with the built-in chuckle. Her breathing seemed suddenly difficult, the muscles in her chest cruelly tight.
Dear lord, she prayed silently, give me the courage to
get through the next few minutes.

She felt Kevin's hand creep into hers as she watched the door-handle turn. It seemed to take forever. Then her mother was standing in the doorway, the enquiring smile that curved her lips fading slowly away as she looked at Kyla.

Large brown eyes moved dazedly down to Kevin and back again, while Kyla struggled to sort out all the warring emotions that clashed in her own heart. Resentment. Anger. Distrust. Disappointment.

And love.

The wind howled like a ravenous wolf as it rounded the corner, shaking the forsythia branches and tumbling the gnome off the step to roll into the flower-bed below. Kyla ignored it. In one all-encompassing moment, she drank in the sight of this woman who had given her life, and who had then, over twenty years later, unwittingly transformed it into a meaningless agony.

If it weren't for the fine crow's-feet fanning from the corners of her eyes, and the laughter-lines etched around her mouth, Kate Drummond could, at fifty years of age, have been mistaken for a first-year art student. Her brown-fringed eyes were still clear and luminous, her long hair still swung over one shoulder in a saucy black braid, and her petite figure, still sparrow-thin, was attired in its usual Bohemian garb. Her smock, which had once been grey but was now a futuristic palette of purple, sky blue and cherry red paint, swirled atop legs encased in black twill drainpipes smudged with white. Despite the draughtiness of the old house, her feet—nails glossed with cherry varnish—were unstockinged, and encased in a pair of flat black leather sandals. And everywhere was jewellery. . .from her dainty lobes tinkled several silver hoops the size of cartwheels, around her neck hung linked silver chains, and displayed on the fingers that were now being pressed against parted red lips in a gesture of disbelief were rings encrusted with glittering coloured gems.

On anyone else, it would have looked tawdry, garish. On Kathleen O'Malley Drummond, it looked just fine.

All the homesickness of five years gushed to the surface as she heard her mother say, 'Holy Mother of God, it's really you——' Kyla had never seen her mother cry before. 'You've come home. Oh, it's more than I ever expected, more than I——'

The scent of her mother's favourite Midnight in Paris enveloped Kyla as she was drawn into the thin, strong arms, the taste of her mother's tears salty on her lips as she brushed the fragrantly powdered cheeks with a kiss. It was a sweet agony. Oh, how she wished her mother could have stayed on her pedestal forever, wished that her own heart wasn't torn with the anguish of knowing too much. . .

Kyla gulped back a noisy sob as she and Kevin were pulled inside. . .a sob that changed into a teary, shaky laugh as she smelled the familiar aromas of home. Not in this house the fragrance of lemon polish or winter roses; not the smell of scones baking or fruit in a silver basket. . .

'I don't believe it!' Her voice wavered with emotion. 'It smells like. . .Oh, my heavens, Kate, he's still at it!'

Kate took a Kleenex from one voluminous pocket of her smock. She tried to speak, but shook her head helplessly as she dabbed at the tears streaming down her cheeks.

The air was pungent with a nostril-twitching mixture of sulphur, burning rubber, and something else that Kyla couldn't quite define. 'For pete's sake, Kate,' she spluttered weakly, 'what's Dad up to this time?'

'I'll tell you all about your father's latest invention over a cup of tea.' Her mother scrubbed her eyes fiercely. 'First,' she finally managed a tremulous smile, 'let me have a look at this darlin' boy.'

Kyla pushed back Kevin's fur-trimmed hood. 'This is your Grandma, sweetheart. Shake hands and say "Hi".'

She barely heard her mother's 'Welcome to Tigh Na Mara, my dear little lamb,' as she hugged Kevin, or his politely whispered, 'Hi, Grandma,' so busy was she looking around the brightly lit hallway with its faded brown and cream striped wallpaper and scarred mahogany hallstand.

'Where's. . .where's everyone?'

She had been about to say 'Where's Nairne?' but somehow her sister's name had stuck in her throat. She bent down to unzip Kevin's jacket, but he said quietly, 'I'll do it myself.'

Her mother didn't answer, and Kyla got up from her crouching position and was startled when she glanced at her mother's face. She was staring at Kyla with such a look of sorrow that Kyla almost cried out. But, as quickly as it had appeared, it was gone. It had only been there for a second. Already Kyla wondered if she had just imagined it. It was a look as if. . .she swallowed, as an unthinkable thought crossed her mind. . .as if she knew the real reason why Kyla had married Drew. Oh, no, Kyla thought, that was impossible. It couldn't be. . .

But weren't Kate's slender, artistic fingers shaking as she toyed with one of her silver hoop earrings?

'Kate?' Kyla slid off her coat and hung it on the hallstand, then took Kevin's from him and did the same. 'What's——'

'Your father's upstairs.' Her mother rushed her words, as if unwilling to let Kyla finish her question. 'Nairne should be back any minute. She's gone out with. . .' She hesitated, and Kyla thought she saw a flush colour the fine high cheekbones. 'She's gone out with——'

'Kyla! Love!'

An exuberant shout filled the small hallway, and with one last, frowning glance at her mother Kyla forgot everything else as a larger-than-life figure—a tornado with a shock of ginger hair and beard to match— thundered down the stairs three at a time, scooping up

Kevin and somehow at the same time managing to embrace Kyla in a bone-crushing bear-hug. 'I heard voices. . .I thought I was dreaming. But no, Kyla, not a dream this time. It's really you. I thought you'd never come home.'

Horn-rimmed glasses brushed against Kyla's ear, the smell of peppermint from her father's breath and sulphur from his clothes filling her nostrils as she put her arms round Malcolm Drummond's hefty back, and she found her fingers gripping his red and green tartan shirt as if she'd never let go.

Their embrace could have lasted only ten seconds at most, but with it Kyla expressed all the fierce, unreserved love she felt for her father. Once upon a time, she had known the same kind of love for her mother, but now there was an invisible wall between them. . .a wall erected by Kyla herself.

'And this is Kevin. My, what a fine wee man you are, too!' He dropped his grandson gently to the floor and draped a heavy arm round Kyla's shoulders. 'Such a lot of water's gone under the bridge since you were here last. You got yourself married, and had a son, and lost your husband forbye. You've had a hard row to hoe.' Blue eyes that were usually vague and misty, like the hazy blue of Loch Craig on a summer's day, were glistening as they searched Kyla's face. 'My, but you're a sight for sore eyes. Tell me, lass, how does it feel to be back in Glencraig?'

Kyla smiled through her tears as her father, in his inimitable fashion, spouted one cliché after another. She winked in answer to her mother's rolled eyes before saying, with a teasing smile, 'I'm glad, Dad. It didn't take me long to find out that I'd left the clover for the heather. Toronto may be a fine city, but it's not my cup of tea. There's no place like home!'

The old grandfather clock at the curve of the stairs chimed the hour melodiously, and Malcolm swivelled round, a startled look on his bearded face. 'Glory be, but the time flies!' He reached one hairy hand out to Kevin. 'Come away through with me and see your old Grandad's workshop. We'll let the womenfolk have some time on their own to get over all their crying and hugging. I'm working on something that's going to be the most important discovery since plastic, and I have to add my own secret ingredient right now. . .'

Kevin looked up at Kyla with wide hazel eyes, appearing to be completely mesmerised by this great bear of a man with the orange beard.

'It's OK, sweetie,' she said, giving him a gentle push. 'You go and see what Grandad's working on.'

Kyla watched with her lips twisted in an anxious grimace as Kevin laid down his Lego case. Placing his hand almost mechanically in his grandfather's, he allowed himself to be led away to the workshop at the back of the house.

'He'll be all right. They should get to know each other,' Kate said reassuringly, as she tucked the case out of the way. 'And you know how good your dad is with children. Now, let's go in and sit by the fire.'

They walked into the living-room, and Kyla found herself moving automatically to the window, where she stood looking out into the twilight—at the view of the loch she'd have given a million dollars to see when she lived in the neat suburban house in Toronto.

'We were sorry that we couldn't be here for Barclay's funeral yesterday.' Kate had come up to stand beside her. 'It——' She paused and tilted her head sideways as if listening. 'Oh, saints preserve us, there's that dratted phone! D'ye mind, dear? I'll be back in the shake of a rat's tail.' Flicking her braid behind her back, she gave Kyla a quick hug and darted out of the room, leaving behind the lingering fragrance of her perfume.

A part from the occasional shriek of the gale outside, there was no sound in the small room. Even the coals in the hearth were still, with no sparking logs or hissing flames, just a warm, red glow. In the hushed quiet, Kyla could hear the echo of her mother's words: 'We were sorry we couldn't be here for Barclay's funeral yesterday.' With a bitterness that surprised her, she wondered how her mother could so casually have mentioned Barclay Ferguson's name, as if he were nothing but an old family friend. After what had happened between them—even if it was so long ago—surely there should have been at least a hint of embarrassment in her mother's voice?

Turning away from the window, Kyla pushed the disturbing thought aside. There was no place now for bitterness. Not if she truly wanted Kevin and herself to become part of this family. And of course she did, so the past, no matter how dreadful, had to be left behind.

She felt as if she were a stranger in her childhood home. In earlier days, she'd have followed her mother to the kitchen, put on the kettle for a cup of tea, chatted happily about anything and everything. But even though she was now a guest. . .and an uninvited one, at that. . .she was glad to be on her own to wander around the drawing-room unobserved.

She couldn't help smiling as she walked across the faded red and navy carpeting, stopping to run her fingers over the carved gate-leg table against one wall and pausing to examine the old-fashioned TV set which she remembered from five years ago. Leaning over the hearth, she inspected the objects on the mantelpiece—family photographs in their old frames and cherished ornaments that had been made by herself and Nairne when they were at school.

Be it ever so humble, she thought, feeling her eyes begin to fill with tears.

Embarrassed by the surge of emotion, she brushed the back of her hand over her eyes and, with a sniff, bent to lift the poker and prod the quietly glowing coals into more vivid life.

And, just as she returned the poker to its place on the companion set, she heard the back door slam shut.

With a muffled exclamation, she straightened herself, her cheeks flushed from the heat of the fire. Her fingers shook as she brushed back the long strands of hair that had fallen forward, and almost without realising what she was doing she took up a stance on the fireside rug, facing the door, her hands thrust into the deep pockets of her charcoal-grey skirt to hide their trembling.

Somehow she knew that Nairne would come straight into the drawing-room, and all at once the surges of nausea started again. She withdrew her hands from her pockets and folded her arms beneath her breasts, feeling her nails dig into her skin as she clutched her sides.

It flashed through her mind that this was the way someone might feel when awaiting the firing squad. Her head felt light and her legs useless, as if she'd been ill in bed for weeks. She fixed her gaze on the door-handle, all her senses intensified. Her mother's Midnight in Paris was chokingly thick in her nostrils, the lilting sound of her sister's voice right outside the door almost painful in her ear.

Nairne was calling to somebody, in a light and teasing tone.

'You'd forget your head if it wasn't fixed on!' Her merry chuckle tinkled through the air. 'Yes, I agree, that *is* important. Hurry up, then, I'll be waiting for you.'

Kyla was too wound up to wonder who her sister was talking to. She felt as if every single nerve-ending in her entire body were prickling. Her emotions were screamingly tangled with each other. . .love for her sister inextricably twisted with anxiety, her longing to see the younger girl laced with the incredible pain of having hurt her so very much.

And then the door opened, and the sound of Nairne's merry laughter preceded her into the room.

Kyla felt her spine stiffen as her sister made a swirling entrance, singing happily in a low voice. . .till she suddenly realised that she wasn't alone. The song died in her throat, her hands flew to her neck, and Kyla could hear her strangled gasp right across the room.

'*Kyla*!' Huge pansy-blue eyes gazed round the room desperately, as if looking for a way to escape. 'How did you get here? I didn't know you were coming. . .nobody told me. . .'

All Kyla could do was stare as a flush that was the deep red of a peony rose spread upwards from the base of her sister's throat to cover her cheeks. This was Nairne? It was unbelievable. The seventeen-year-old with the pretty oval face and short fair hair was now, at twenty-two, a stunningly attractive woman.

Kyla stared with an aching heart at the wild, tangled curls that tumbled over Nairne's shoulders like a cascade of golden, freshly minted coins, gazed in surprise at the full breasts, tiny waist and long, elegant legs. Her lips were shining with peach gloss, her eyes accentuated with denim-blue shadow the same colour as her V-necked wool sweater and skin-tight jeans.

Kyla didn't realise she'd been holding her breath till her chest suddenly felt constricted with pain. 'Oh, Nairne, it's so good to see you.' Her voice trembled as she took a tentative step forward. 'I'm sorry I gave you such a shock. You didn't know that I'd come home for Barclay's funeral?'

She halted abruptly as Nairne flinched away from her, her slender body falling against the door, snapping it shut.

'Yes, I knew you were back.' The younger girl spoke on a shuddering indrawn breath. 'But I. . .I didn't expect. . .I didn't think you'd be coming here. Not to Tigh Na Mara.'

There was a long frozen moment as they stared at each other. Kyla could have screamed with frustration as she crushed back the longing to rush to her sister and take her in her arms. But she knew that it was far, far too soon for that. The very sight of her must have brought back memories that were almost too painful to bear.

The pain of betrayal. Was there any other pain as wounding?

'You're looking great, Nairne.' Kyla's voice was husky with emotion when finally she spoke. She tried to smile, but her lips trembled disobediently. 'You've really grown up——'

A mirthless laugh filled the space between them. 'Oh, I've grown up all right.' The lilting voice Kyla had heard outside the door earlier was now harsh. 'I had to, didn't I? And in a hurry, too. But of course, you didn't wait around to see!' Nairne's nostrils flared white, her translucent skin tightened over her cheekbones, emphasising the peppering of cinnamon-coloured freckles. 'But I suppose I should thank you. I could laugh now, when I remember what a romantic twit I was! I must admit, though, that it was a hard lesson to learn—that people aren't what they seem. But I couldn't have had a more appropriate teacher, could I?' Her lips twisted scornfully. 'Who better to teach you about deceit than the person you trust the most?'

Now it was Kyla's turn to flinch, but Nairne wasn't finished yet. Flicking her reddish-gold curls away from her face with the back of one hand, she confronted Kyla with eyes that were hostile and defiant.

'And what, dear sister, has brought you to Tigh Na Mara this stormy day?'

Kyla met her gaze evenly, but for a moment couldn't reply because of the tightness of her throat. Nairne still leaned against the door, but, whereas before she had done so to support herself against the shock of seeing her sister, Kyla was aware that she was now trying to appear nonchalant. She knew that Nairne felt anything but nonchalant. She had seen the unsteadiness of her fingers, heard the tears lurking behind the accusing words.

Kyla wondered fleetingly if Nairne had bottled up all her feelings of hurt and betrayal five years ago. Was there anyone in whom she might have confided? Kyla almost shook her head. No, she didn't think so. She had been too sensitive, too shy to spill out her heart to anyone. Up till that time, Kyla herself had been her only confidante.

Nairne had always had a gentle, forgiving nature; she had never been one to hold a grudge. No doubt, thought Kyla, there was a battle going on inside her, right at this moment, as she tried to balance the seventeen years of love they had shared against the remembrance of what Kyla had done.

Kyla sighed as she saw Nairne's lips tighten grimly. It was going to take longer than she had thought. And it was going to take all the patience, all the passion she had, to win Nairne over, teach her that it was safe to trust her again.

A coal fell out on to the hearth, and Kyla started, then quickly turned to lift it with the tongs from the companion set. As she did, she heard the door-handle turn, heard her mother say, 'Oh, sorry, darling, I didn't know you were standing right there.' She looked from one to the other, her brown eyes wary. 'You found Kyla. . .' She hesitated, as if about to say more, but thinking better of it. Her silver hoops glinted in the light. 'We can all talk later. Meantime,' she took Nairne's hand in hers and rubbed it affectionately against her own cheek, casting an anxious glance into the pale, freckled face, 'I was looking for you. I *thought* I heard you come in. . .Rory's on the phone for you. Would you take it? The kettle's almost boiling, Kyla. I'll just be another few minutes.' As she spoke, she looked around the room, her arched black eyebrows raised quizzically. 'I thought you were bringing. . .' Her words trailed away, and for just a second her glance slid uneasily to her elder daughter, before settling on Nairne again.

'Yes, he's coming, Mum.' Nairne's voice was muffled as, tearing her gaze from Kyla, she followed her mother into the hallway but Kyla heard her say, 'He's gone back to town. He forgot——'

The door shut, and Kyla sank lifelessly into one of the armchairs, her head in her hands as tears welled in her eyes. It was so much worse than she had ever imagined. Something was very wrong, and she had no idea what it was. Something more than just her unexpected return to Tigh Na Mara.

She swept her damp hair from her tear-stained cheeks, and looked unseeingly into the fire as she tried to sort out the tumultuous thoughts swirling round and round in her head.

It was no surprise that Nairne had rejected her first attempt at a reconciliation. Her reaction was more or less as Kyla had anticipated it.

So was her father's. Malcolm Drummond, who was always so wrapped up in his inventions that the rest of the world passed him by, had accepted her return as a delightful surprise. If he had ever wondered why Kyla had jilted Adam to marry Drew, it would have been just in passing. His outlook on life was childlike, innocent, uncomplicated. He saw only the good in everybody.

But Kate. . .Kate was the one who was acting out of character. She had always been equally fond of her two girls, so why was she being so. . .so *nice* to her? Why wasn't there an undercurrent of reserve, as if she wanted to let Kyla know, if not in so many words, that what she had done to Nairne five years ago wasn't just something that could be brushed under the rug as if it had never happened? Kyla shuddered. The only explanation would be if she had guessed Kyla's reason for stealing Drew from her sister, and guessed that she had done it because the alternative. . .to let Nairne and Drew marry. . .was *unthinkable*!

Kyla let her head fall back against the flower-embroidered chair-back. She must be wrong. No one in the whole world knew that she had overheard the telephone conversation between Kate and Barclay Ferguson.

There was no doubt that Kate was absolutely delighted to have Kyla home. *Why, then, was she on pins?*

As Kyla stood up and wiped away the last of her tears, she wished that she could as easily wipe away the ominous feeling that she wasn't going to have to wait too long to find out.

CHAPTER FOUR

'Is THAT someone at the front door?' Kate's head cocked questioningly to one side as she held the willow-pattern teapot over Nairne's cup. 'Yes, I think——'

'I'll get it.' Touching her napkin to her mouth, Nairne got up abruptly from the chesterfield and walked with a swift, graceful stride across the room. 'Don't pour me any more tea, Mum, I've had enough, thanks.'

'It'll probably be——'

Whatever Kate had been going to say was interrupted as Kevin and his grandfather entered the room. Kyla laid her cup on the coffee-table and stood up, her legs wobbly. Oh, how could she have forgotten about this, forgotten that Nairne and Kevin still had to meet?

Her sister had come to a halt, standing transfixed as Kevin sidled over to his mother. It was a measure of comfort to scoop him up and cuddle his warm, thin body against her breast. He twined his arms round her neck, and peeked shyly at Nairne.

Kyla's heart ached as she saw the expression on her sister's face. The pansy-blue eyes looked bruised, the freckled skin was pale as parchment, the peach-glossed lips quivering. Oh, I can't stand it, Kyla thought, as she frantically crushed down the wild urge to pour out the truth to Nairne. . .anything to wipe out that anguished, wounded expression.

Kyla watched helplessly as her sister approached them. She walked slowly, as if pushed against her will by an invisible hand. A faint floral fragrance drifted into Kyla's nostrils as Nairne's fine-boned fingers reached out to touch Kevin's smooth cheek—fingers that trembled as they caressed the child of the man she had once hoped to marry. The man who had been so callously stolen from her.

'He looks like. . .looks like Drew.' Nairne's tangled cloud of hair fell like a ripple of old gold over her cheeks, hiding her eyes. 'He's darling.' Without once letting her glance fall on Kyla, she pivoted on her heel and said merrily to her parents, 'Isn't he? What do you think of your grandson, Dad?'

Despair trickled through Kyla's veins, threatening to wash away all her hopes of winning Nairne over. Had her expectations been far too high? Had she set herself an impossible task?

She thought she heard a sob as Nairne rushed out without waiting for her father to answer, but, before she could make up-her mind if she was right, Kate was sitting her down again, with Kevin curled up on the armchair beside her, urging her to have another of Albert the Baker's cream buns.

'It was Rory Campbell who was on the phone for Nairne.' Kate sat up straight on the edge of the chesterfield, busying herself with the teapot as she tumbled into conversation in an obvious effort to ease the tension. 'He's her boss. She's been working for——'

'Nairne working?' In all the years Kyla had been away, she had foolishly imagined that time had stood still in Glencraig. She had pictured her sister just as she'd been at seventeen. It was stupid, she knew, yet that was how it was. Nairne had always been a home bird, working around the house, doing the chores that Kate, so busy with her painting, tended to neglect. 'I didn't know——'

'Your sister's a social worker.' There was no mistaking the pride in Malcolm Drummond's voice as he talked about his younger daughter. He had been throwing a shovelful of coal on to the fire; now he lowered his solid body into the deep armchair across from Kyla. 'She went away to do her training. . .just after you left for Canada.'

Kyla felt her eyelids flicker as he referred to that time, but, though Kate's teacup clattered slightly on her saucer, Malcolm gave no sign of knowing that he'd said anything untoward. 'Said she needed a change,' he went on. 'Went to university in Edinburgh, and did very well. When she came back to Glencraig, Rory hired her to work with him at the Glencraig Youth Centre.'

Kyla blinked in amazement. She was finding that some things had changed indeed in the last five years. Her baby sister was now a rare beauty. . .and a successful social worker into the bargain. The pride in Kyla's voice echoed the pride in her father's. 'That's great! I'm impressed.'

'Perhaps she'd never have done it if you had stayed here.' Kate played with the curl at the end of her black braid, not looking at Kyla. 'She worshipped you. You were a secretary at Ferguson Whisky, so that's probably what she'd have wanted to be too. And——'

'The laddie'll soon be in the land of Nod.'

Kyla twisted her head to look at Kevin's face as her father interrupted whatever Kate had been about to say. Sure enough, his eyes were growing heavy, the lashes feathering his flushed cheeks.

'It's been too much excitement for him for one day,' she said, dropping a kiss on the pale forehead. 'Don't drop off yet, honey. Try to stay awake till I get you back to Glencraig House——'

'Can't you put him down here? In your old bed?' Kate's rings glittered as she pointed up to the ceiling. 'Then you can stay for dinner.'

A family dinner. How she'd have loved to stay. But it was too soon; it would be awkward, with Nairne pretending that her elder sister wasn't there. . . 'Thanks, it's kind of you, Kate, but I know Martha will have our meal ready——'

'I want to go home.' Kevin snuggled his head against Kyla's neck as he whispered in her ear.

'We're just going, Kev.' Kyla threw an apologetic smile at her parents. 'Can we take a rain-check?'

As the door opened, Kyla found herself thinking wryly that Tigh Na Mara was just as it had always been, with people popping in and out of rooms like actors in a French farce. And then her lips parted in a dismayed gasp. Nairne had come back, and with her she had brought the last person on earth that Kyla had expected to see. He was tall, and dark, and very, very handsome in his red sweater and jeans. The sight of him made Kyla dizzy; she was glad she was sitting down.

'Adam!' Malcolm levered himself from his seat, and crossed the room, hand outstretched to Adam as Nairne slid past him and went to stand behind the sofa.

Kyla tried to steady herself, finally understanding the reason for Kate's earlier uneasiness. She had known that Nairne was bringing Adam to Tigh Na Mara that afternoon, and Kyla's unexpected arrival had thrown the cat among the pigeons.

But *Adam* had known she was going to be here; hadn't she herself been the one to tell him? 'This afternoon we're going to Tigh Na Mara.' So why was he here? What was he playing at? What did he expect to gain by forcing his company on her? She'd have thought he'd have moved heaven and earth to avoid seeing her when he hated her as much as he did.

'You can see that the prodigal's returned.' Malcolm's voice boomed into the room, filling every corner. 'But maybe you had a few words with her yesterday, at the funeral. . .'

'Aye, that I did.' Adam avoided looking at Kyla, apparently concentrating all his attention on the small silver salver he was balancing on the palm of one hand at shoulder level. 'I did manage to say a couple of words to her, just before I left.'

If Kyla could have blushed, she would. She knew only

too well which two words Adam was referring to: 'Gold-digging *bitch!*' Oh, he was cruel. Not content with insulting her once, he was getting double coverage by reminding her of his taunt when she couldn't speak out to defend herself. Despite the fact that he hadn't looked at her once since he'd come in, the tension sizzled between them so strongly, she wondered why the air wasn't filled with sparks and blue smoke!

Malcolm and Kevin seemed unaware of any undercurrents, but Kate was sitting up rigidly with her hands to her face—which now seemed to be her reaction to any situation she couldn't handle, Kyla thought wryly. Nairne's fingers were curled tautly over the back of the sofa, her face a white, strained mask.

'And what have we got here?' Malcolm's blue eyes sparkled as he looked over his horn-rimmed spectacles at the tray. 'Glasses? And Kate's best Waterford crystal, at that! What kind of wine have you brought us today, Adam, my man?'

'Nairne?' Adam grinned at Nairne and she suddenly came to life.

'Oops, sorry!' She emerged from behind the sofa and Kyla could see a bottle in her hands. 'Not just your ordinary, everyday wine. Champagne, Dad, the best Glencraig has to offer.'

Kyla watched, bemused, as Adam unwound the wrapping from the neck of the bottle. And when his lean, tanned fingers began working on the cork she couldn't take her eyes from them. They were competent, well-shaped. . .skilful. They were the first hands that had ever caressed her naked body, the first hands to. . .

She shivered, and shook her head. There was no point in letting her mind travel in that direction. She sat back wearily, and as she raised her gaze to take in the whole room she knew beyond the shadow of a doubt that the scene would remain in her mind forever. Her father was sitting comfortably in his chair, stroking his red beard;

Kate was on the sofa, her black-sheathed legs curled up under her, one hand winding her plait round the top of her head. Kevin had perked up at the explosive pop of the bottle, and Nairne was hunting behind the chester-field for the cork, with only her back visible.

Adam was pouring champagne into the shallow crystal glasses with a triumphant expression lightening his grey eyes.

A Norman Rockwell painting, Kyla thought. A stranger looking in would surely muse, 'What a happy family. . .'

She closed her eyes to shut out the pain, and when she opened them Adam was watching her. Their gazes clashed, and a charge of electricity sparked between them. Kyla realised that his spiteful, malicious sneer of the morning was gone. The transformation was incred-ible. His eyes were twinkling, and laughter-lines fanned from the corners. His beautiful sensual mouth was curved in a smile that was warm and disarming. And it was a smile that was undoubtedly directed at her.

Her head spun so that she scarcely heard the cheerful babble of sound as he finished filling the glasses, pouring only a thimbleful into the sixth.

'A time to celebrate.' A dark lock of hair fell over his forehead, taking years off him. His warm, magnetic aura filled the room as he gestured widely. 'Here we are. Kate, Nairne, Kyla. . .Malcolm, Kevin. . .Now, it's time for us to drink a toast.'

He's going to welcome me home.

Kyla felt a tiny flame of warmth kindle in a corner of her heart. Was it possible? Was it going to be as easy as this? Did miracles really happen?

She crushed back the joy that started to surge up inside her, knowing how vulnerable she was, and unwill-ing to risk disappointment.

But as she looked around she could see that even Nairne had lost her strained expression, and was smiling.

She had moved to stand by Adam's side. Far taller than Kyla, her chin was level with his shoulders and she had tilted it up to him, her hair a burnished cloud around her lovely, intelligent face. She was looking at him with eyes that were soft with tenderness, with caring, with——

Just as Adam raised his glass to propose the toast, Kyla knew. There was no time for a sudden twinge of alarm, a quick premonition, an element of uncertainty.

Inside her a protesting voice screamed, so loudly that she thought surely they must all turn and stare at her. But no one heard. She hadn't made a sound.

And now all she could do was watch, and listen, and feel—feel the lifeblood seeping from her heart as Adam's voice rang in her ears. It echoed round and round in circles, till her head felt as if it were filled with the agony of it.

'Drink with me, everyone, as I propose a toast to the most faithful friend in the world.' He put out an arm and pulled a radiant Nairne into the curve of his shoulders, right up against his heart, her hair gleaming like a splash of yellow sunlight against the vivid tulip red of his sweater.

'Folks, Nairne and I want you to be the first to hear our wonderful news. We're going to be married.'

'I'll only be gone for an hour or so. Just want to go out for a walk in the dark, let the wind blow some of the cobwebs away. Are you sure you won't mind listening for Kevin?'

'There's no need to whisper, missy. He's dead to the world. I don't know what you were thinking of, letting Adam fill him with champagne this afternoon!'

'He didn't *fill* him, Martha. He barely gave him enogh to wet his lips. It was. . .' Kyla bent to tuck in Kevin's blankets, though she had already folded them cosily up to his chin. 'It was kind of Adam to want everyone to

share in the good news, and very thoughtful of him not
to leave Kevin out.'

'Aye.' Martha walked to the bedroom door and held it
open for Kyla. Kyla could feel the calculating green eyes
scrutinising her face as she passed and walked out into
the hallway. 'Aye, Adam Garvie's a nice man.' The
housekeeper shuffled across the landing, and Kyla could
hear her wheezy breath, smell the stale tobacco from her
cardigan. She preceded Kyla down the stairs, not saying
any more till they were both down in the hallway. 'So
he's got himself engaged, and to your sister Nairne.
Well, I wonder at him. I had figured him out for a one-
woman man, as they say. After you jilted the puir lad, I
thought he'd go to his grave a bachelor.'

Kyla turned away, hoping Martha couldn't see the
way her lips were trembling. As she reached to the
hallstand for her three-quarter-length navy wool jacket,
Martha went on, 'I never could understand why you
threw him over. Och, Drew was a fine young man in his
own way. . .a wheen spoiled, maybe, not having a
mother since he was a young bairn. . .but he was never
a patch on Garvie of Redhillock.'

Kyla bent to pull on her high leather boots, feeling
overcome all at once by the events of the day. She had
managed to tell Martha what had transpired at Tigh Na
Mara without, she hoped, giving away her feelings of
shock. But she couldn't keep up her poised demeanour
much longer. If Martha insisted on probing, she might
break down altogether. And that wouldn't do. She
mustn't do anything that might risk Nairne's newfound
happiness. She tried to deny the tangled feelings that
were torturing her and concentrate on being happy for
her sister. After the misery Nairne had gone through,
she had at last found a real love to make up for the one
that had been stolen from her. It was wonderful, after all
these years, all the heartbreak, that things should have
turned out so well for her and Adam. They deserved it,

after they had been so humiliated, so rejected. . .so betrayed.

Kyla twisted her red scarf round her ncek. 'A bachelor?' She managed a soft laugh. 'Apparently not, Martha. He's not going to be a bachelor for much longer. They're planning a June wedding.' Holding the edge of the door with both hands, she looked over her whitened knuckles into Martha's avid eyes. 'Now, the sooner I go, the sooner I'll be back. How about having a cup of tea ready?'

She flung a smile in Martha's direction as she slipped out into the pitch-darkness.

Crazy! was her first thought as the wind caught at her throat, making her gasp. What normal person would go out for a walk on a night like this?

But she didn't feel normal; not tonight.

The primal scent of the earth filled her nostrils, along with the clean, tangy fragrance of the sea wind from the north as it tangled through her long hair.

Now that her eyes were used to the night, she realised it wasn't pitch-black, as she had thought. There was a bit of a moon; she could see it through the bare, swaying branches of the beech trees. The gnarled arms reached and dipped, like a chorus line of ageing dancers.

Kyla hesitated for a moment as she emerged from the tree-lined drive. If she followed the back road it would take her into Glencraig. She didn't want to go towards the town; someone might stop and offer her a ride. She turned her head and looked down the glen. About a mile away, its lights sparkling in the dark, was Redhillock Farm. The path ran along the edge of the loch; she knew it like the back of her hand. There was no chance of meeting anyone there on a night like this; she would go almost to the house and back. That should get her blood pulsing again, put some colour in her pale cheeks and help her to sleep.

She had literally reeled from the shock of hearing that

Adam and Nairne were engaged. She had stayed at Tigh
Na Mara only long enough to drink the couple's health,
but her mind had been in a whirl of bewilderment.

Buried in her unhappy thoughts, Kyla didn't realise
that she was close to Redhillock till she was right at the
front garden gate. There were no great beech trees here,
only one giant oak at the side of the road, and Kyla
leaned gratefully against it, glad to shelter from the wind
for a minute before turning to go back.

She wished she'd stopped to put on a pair of gloves,
but she'd been in too much of a hurry to get away from
Martha and her questions. Rubbing her ice-cold hands
together, she stared at the outline of the long, low
farmhouse which at one time she had thought would be
her home for the rest of her life. Now it was to be
Nairne's home. If she and her sister eventually recon-
ciled, she would visit here with Kevin. Could she bear
it? Had she made a ghastly mistake in coming back?

She let herself slide down against the rough bark,
pulling the back of her jacket under her bottom as she
crouched on top of a huge root, curling into a ball to
protect herself from the wind. Looking up at the moon
through the network of branches, she found herself
remembering the last day she had spent in the glen,
remembering how she had found out the shocking truth
about Kate and Barclay Ferguson. . .

She had been sitting in her office at Ferguson Whisky,
in her typist's chair by the window, stretching her arms
out in front of her in an effort to relax the tension
knotting in her neck after a particularly hard day. Her
In basket was empty, the Out basket piled high with
letters for posting. Thank goodness it was time to go
home; Adam was taking her out for dinner, as he did
every Friday night.

The antique engagement ring he'd given her the week
before—a huge ruby in an unusual and intricate silver

setting—caught the light from the late afternoon sun, refracting it, making the precious stone shimmer and flash hypnotically. Just as Adam's eyes did when——

'Ye're still here, lassie?'

Kyla swivelled her chair round with a gasp as Barclay's gruff, broadly accented voice came from the doorway. She smiled sheepishly; he'd probably seen her admiring the way the ring looked on her long, neatly manicured finger.

'I'm just going, Mr Ferguson.' She stood up and brushed a piece of lint from her Drummond tartan skirt. 'I finished a few minutes ago.'

Embarrassed, she scooped up the letters and bent to tuck them into her bucket bag on the floor at her feet, just giving him a brief glance. His tall, well-proportioned figure was leaning against the door-jamb casually, and there was no mistaking the teasing twinkle in his eyes. 'Dreaming about your wedding day, I dare say?'

Kyla was just about to reply, when she saw a flash of fair hair behind Barclay, and a pair of dark, pansy-blue eyes peeking over the shoulder of his well-cut grey suit.

'Oops, sorry, Mr Ferguson. I didn't expect you'd still be here. I just wanted to see Kyla. . .'

As Barclay stepped aside, Nairne slid past him with a murmured 'excuse me', her navy school tunic rumpled, her white blouse open at the neck, her red and navy striped tie askew. She looked around, her pale face flushed with excitement. 'Last day of school—and the most wonderful day of my life! Oh, Kyla, wait till I tell you my news!'

Kyla bit back a smile of astonishment. Was this the shy, introverted Nairne she thought she knew so well? To think she would let herself go like this in front of Barclay Ferguson was mind-boggling.

'Well, I'll be on my way. Enjoy your weekend, Kyla. And Nairne. . .enjoy the first day of the rest of your life.' Barclay chuckled as he turned away.

'Oh, wait, Mr Ferguson.' Nairne, suddenly quieter, appealed to him to stay. 'My news. . .well, it concerns you too, in a way. . .'

Kyla watched in amazement as her sister, long, navy-stockinged legs astride, blushed to the roots of her fair hair. 'I know this'll be a surprise to you both. It was to me, too. But, well. . .there's never been any secret about the way I felt about Drew. Ever since we were small. . .' She pivoted round so that she was facing her sister. 'He came to meet me after school. Oh, I know you'll hardly believe this. . .after all, I'm only seventeen, though I *will* be eighteen very soon. . .but——'

She beamed, her small, intelligent features radiant. '*Drew proposed to me.* Kyla,' she tossed her fringe off her forehead impatiently, 'he wants us to have a double wedding!'

Kyla was too stunned to speak. Drew had declared his love for her over and over again since he was sixteen, despite her repeatedly telling him she'd never love him in that way. She knew he had been devastated when she and Adam announced their engagement. Oh, lord, she hoped he hadn't turned to Nairne on the rebound. Or was it possible that, knowing that Kyla was finally out of his reach for good, he'd looked at Nairne and seen her for the first time in a different light?

'Excuse me, I——'

Her eyes widened as she glanced at Barclay. Good lord, but he looked ill. His rugged, attractive features were drawn, and an unhealthy yellow tinged his usually pink-toned skin.

'I'm sorry, Nairne. . .we'll talk later.' He was obviously finding it difficult to speak. 'I feel a bit tired—a heavy day, as Kyla will tell you. I'll go and sit down, put my feet on the desk for ten minutes. . .'

His footsteps had a hollow ring as he walked away down the hallway, and the sound of his door shutting echoed in the sudden silence of Kyla's office.

'Was it me? Was it because he doesn't want me to marry Drew?' Nairne's voice trembled tearfully, her joy dissipated like the bubbles in a glass of flat chanpagne. 'Oh, Kyla, if——'

'No, of course not.' Kyla lifted her bag and put a firm, reassuring arm round Nairne's shoulders. 'He probably ate too much at lunchtime and has a touch of indigestion.'

But as they walked out into the sunshine she sneaked a worried glance back along the hallway towards Barclay's room. 'I think your news is just wonderful.' She gave her sister a distracted hug. 'It's going to take me some time to get used to it, though! My baby sister, engaged to be married. And a double wedding. . .what a fantastic idea. When is Drew going to give you your ring?'

She tried to listen as Nairne prattled on happily about her love for Drew. 'You know, Kyla, he hasn't even kissed me yet. But it doesn't matter. And I know how he's always had a thing for you. But I feel that now he knows it's hopeless, I can make him love me as much as I've always loved him——'

Kyla sighed. It was no use; she had to go back and find out if Barclay was all right. He really had turned a ghastly colour—as if he were going to have a heart attack or something. She'd try to do it without upsetting Nairne. . .

'Oh, dash! Nairne, I've forgotten my bag and I've got some letters to post.' She expelled her breath thankfully as she realised she *did* have a good reason for returning to the office building. 'You go ahead, my bike's round the corner by the rose garden. Sit and wait for me in the sun. I'll just be a sec.'

As she scurried in her soft-soled shoes past her own office, she heard her phone ring. She hesitated, one hand on the wall, leaning in the open doorway. She could see that the light was blinking opposite Barclay's number on the little switchboard. Was he still in the building? Perhaps he wasn't feeling well enough to answer his phone. She ran across the room and lifted the handset from its cradle. Holding it to her ear, she opened her mouth to say, 'Ferguson Whisky, Kyla speaking,' when Barclay's voice came on the line.

'Ferguson here.'

Kyla grimaced—she hated answering the phone when Barclay had already picked it up—and was just on the point of replacing the handset when she heard a frantic, '*Barclay, what are we going to do?*'

Kyla's hand froze in mid-air. It was her mother—her husky Irish accent was unmistakable—and she sounded uncharacteristically distraught. Kyla knew she shouldn't be listening, it was quite unlike her, but she just had to find out why her mother was so upset.

The usual built-in chuckle was conspicuously absent as the familiar voice rushed on, 'You've heard the news? You've got to put a stop to it, right away. Barclay, why didn't you tell me what was going on?'

'Dammit, Kate, calm down. Don't you think it was as much of a shock to me, too?' Though Barclay was just down the hall, his harsh tones seemed a million miles away. 'We've got to think. . .'

She frowned in bewilderment. Her mother and Barclay Ferguson were obviously discussing the fact that Drew had proposed to Nairne. She could understand why Barclay might be upset; after all, Drew was only nineteen, and though he would come into a fair bit of money when he reached twenty-one, money left him by his mother, he had just recently begun working at Ferguson Whisky, and was hardly in a position to support a wife. But why was Kate so upset? She herself had married at seventeen, and although Malcolm Drummond had been ten years older he had always been a dreamer, working as a fisherman to support his family, but spending all his spare time working on his inventions. Surely she should have been delighted that her younger daughter had landed the most eligible bachelor in Glencraig. . .perhaps even in the whole county?

She felt her stomach heave as her mother's sobbing sounded over the line.

'There's only one thing to do.' Barclay's tone was grim. 'We've got to tell them. Explain to Nairne and Drew exactly what happened.'

Even if Kyla had wanted to, she couldn't have stopped eavesdropping now. Tell them what?

'No!' Kate sounded hysterical. 'No, Barclay. Not that. Oh, I don't care for myself, but it would kill Nairne. She's so young, so idealistic. . .'

Kyla felt her fingers tighten on the black phone.

'There's no alternative, Kate. This engagement has got to be broken. We can not stand by and watch my son marry. . .my. . .oh, hell!'

Kyla felt a shiver slither down her spine as she heard the despair in his voice. Her knees slumped weakly. She didn't understand any of this. What was going on? Barclay couldn't stand by and watch his son marry his. . .his what?

'Kate, we can't stand by and watch my son marry my *daughter*.'

Kyla looked down at the ring on her left hand. The sun was no longer streaming in through the window, but the ruby still glinted, like a pool of blood. She felt her head spin, wondered if her brain had suddenly stopped functioning. She couldn't make any sense of what Barclay was saying. His son marry his. . .daughter? But Barclay didn't have a daughter. Drew had been their only child, his mother had died when he was a toddler, and Barclay had never remarried.

'Barclay, *no one* knows that Nairne is your child— your child and mine. I've never told a soul, not even Mac. . .especially not Mac! After all these years, are we going to have to bring heartbreak to them all—to Mac, to Nairne, to Drew?'

Kyla felt her palms turn cold and clammy, felt as if she were spinning round and round like a top.

Fighting for control, she held her breath as she replaced the handset with infinite care. Just before it settled on the cradle, she heard Barclay's voice in the empty room. 'We'll both sleep on it, Kate. I'll phone you first thing in the morning.'

Panic led speed and stealth to Kyla's flight. She grabbed her bucket bag and ran out of the office with the speed of the wind. She didn't expel her breath till she rounded the corner by the rose beds, and saw that Nairne was gone. A note protruded from the brake lever of her Raleigh. Written in a large, immature hand, it read: 'Can't wait. Too excited. Going home to phone Drew. Love, Nairne.' And, scrawled beneath, a sketch of two brides in long white dresses.

Kyla clambered on to the old bike, looping her bucket bag over the handlebars. She ran right through the 'Stop' sign at the end of the distillery road as she headed for the hill at the head of Loch Craig.

She had to be on her own for a while. She had to have time to think.

A low whimper at her knee interrupted her journey into the past, and she jumped up with a frightened gasp. Flinching back against the huge trunk at her back, trying to discern the source of the noise, she hissed out a relieved sigh. 'Oh, Merle, it's just you, you old rascal!'

Adam's collie—she must be at least fourteen years old now, Kyla thought—must have been prowling around and recognised her scent. Instead of barking in alarm, she was nosing at Kyla's fingers, her tongue warm and rough as it rasped on Kyla's chilled skin. Her tail wagged a friendly greeting, her coat's unusual colouring of blue, grey and black making her almost invisible in the moonlight.

With a teary smile, Kyla crouched down. She hugged the ageing dog and said, 'You remembered me, after all these years. Aren't you faithful, you dear old——'

The wind must have caught her words, and carried them to the man who suddenly materialised beside them. Kyla's startled gaze followed the line of the long, black-clad legs, up over the loose sheepskin jacket, to meet eyes that in the silver light of the moon were devil-dark slits.

The voice was harsh, the face a mask carved out of granite, as the owner of Redhillock Farm ground out with ill-concealed sarcasm, 'Faithful, yes. But I'm surprised that you, Mrs Ferguson, are able to recognise that quality, since you are so singularly lacking in it yourself.'

CHAPTER FIVE

'ADAM!'

Kyla shot up from her crouching position, her heart leaping in alarm as she uttered the protesting exclamation. She had taken it for granted that Adam would stay at Tigh Na Mara for dinner and spend the evening with his new fiancée. It had never crossed her mind that there was any danger of meeting him, despite the fact that she was trespassing on his property.

'What are you doing here?' he demanded roughly. 'Were you looking for me?'

The fresh night wind acted as a go-between, bearing his male scent to her like a personal calling card that brought with it memories of midnight trysts.

Its familiarity choked Kyla, and she stepped back, only to find herself trapped against the thick trunk of the oak tree. She stuffed her cold fingers into the pockets of her jacket. 'No, not looking for you. I needed a breath of air, and didn't want to go towards the town; this was the only alternative. It was too dark to go along any of the paths in the woods, and this track. . .well, I could find my way along here blindfold.'

As soon as she spoke, she realised her mistake and cursed silently. Why couldn't she choose her words more carefully, instead of referring to times that were over? She curled her fingers against her palms as she waited for Adam's reply.

But it wasn't what she had expected. She had been afraid he'd pick up on her remark, and talk about the times they'd strolled the lochside path together, but he didn't. His thoughts were plainly not of the past, but of the present.

'It's as well that we bumped into each other tonight.' Even in the pale light of the moon, she was able to see the strained expression on his face, the rigid set of his body. 'There are things we should discuss, and they're best discussed when no one else can hear.'

He jammed his hands into the pockets of his sheepskin jacket, the clenched fists echoing the grim twist of his lips. 'We have to talk about Nairne.'

If he noticed Kyla's swift intake of breath, he gave no sign. She heard the harsh cry of a bird in the reeds as he went on, 'Nairne's happiness is of the ultimate importance to me. I won't let *anything* spoil it. She's had more than enough heartbreak in her life already—it's only during the last few months that she's begun to approach anything like the happy Nairne that we all used to know.'

Kyla wanted to look away, look anywhere but at his hardened features, his slitted, accusing eyes, but she couldn't. Shadows played on the planes and angles of his lean face, and each shift of his head changed the black and white portrait, creating a series of fascinating, two-tone images. 'We talked, at Tigh Na Mara, after you left.' He turned sideways, abruptly—whether it was that he couldn't bear to look at her, or that he couldn't bear to have her stare so helplessly at him, she couldn't tell. 'We're both prepared to do as you say you want—put the past aside, and act as if it had never happened——'

Kyla fought back a cry of pain. Oh, yes, she had wanted to do that. . .For a long time now, she had wanted to do that. Had wanted to be friends again with Nairne, with Adam. But that was before. . .

Was it too late now? Could she bear to be part of their life, now that they were to be man and wife?

'To that end,' his voice grated into her silent torment, 'you'll be pleased to know that Nairne is going to invite you to be her matron of honour.'

Oh, no, Kyla thought wildly, she couldn't endure it.

Why had she ever come home? She couldn't bite back a pleading cry. 'Oh, no, Adam. I. . .I don't want to. Please. . .I can't. . .'

'Why the hell not?' Adam sounded incredulous—and he had every reason to be. She had made it quite clear that she wanted to forget the past, so why could she not accept Nairne's invitation? Oh, how could she ever admit that the most painful thing in the world for her would be to watch Adam marry someone else?

'It's just that. . .' Her throat tightened and she couldn't go on.

'Just that what?' She jumped as Adam's fingers bit into her arms through the thickness of her jacket. 'Hell, can't you even do *that* for your sister? After all the devastation you caused in her life?' Kyla thought for a moment that he was going to shake her or fling her against the trunk of the tree, but he just swore loudly and dropped his arms in disgust. 'You give an added dimension to the word "selfishness", Mrs Ferguson. You really are something else.'

As Kyla saw the hostility in his eyes, eyes that looked like dark hollows in a white-washed face, she was filled with despair. Her father had said that a lot of water had run under the bridge since she had left, and he had been right. But had there been *too* much? She prayed not, for she had to stay. For Kevin's sake, she had to stay.

She began to shake as the events of the day suddenly caught up with her. Her hands had been cold ever since she'd left Glencraig House; now that icy numbness threatened to spread through her entire body. She had to get away before that happened.

She whirled round, taking him by surprise, and began running back along the path by the loch. Sure-footed as she'd always been, despite her high leather boots, she ran as lightly as the wind. The only sounds she could hear were her ragged panting, and the cracking of twigs beneath her feet.

She had no idea that Adam had started after her. Not until she was half-way along the path and the lights of Glencraig House twinkled up ahead beyond the avenue of beech trees did she hear a heavy step right behind her. She gasped in dismay as strong hands tore at her jacket, swung her round to face him.

'Wait!'

There must have been a root twining its way across the path, hidden by leaves and fir needles. She tripped. Adam lost his balance as he lunged after her, and they fell together on to the moss that bordered the path.

He landed on his back and, as she tried to break free, he pulled her on top of him, his heavy grunt drowning out her protesting gasp.

There were no trees to block out the light of the moon along this curve in the loch edge, and in the silvery glow she could see every feature of Adam's lean face as he lay back on the ground. In the fall, his jacket had been torn open, as had her own. The warmth of his chest against her breasts disturbed her so that she thought she couldn't bear it. For a long moment, they lay motionless, with Kyla's hair falling across her cheeks and over Adam's jaw, the scent of it subtly seductive between them.

Kyla started as his voice, angry and loud above the eerie keening of the wind in the reeds, cut into the tense atmosphere.

'You really are a bitch!'

With a sudden heave of his shoulders he reversed their positions so that he was over her. He grasped her hands and clenched them inside his own, pinned them against the ground at either side of her head. 'Have you no feelings at all?' he grated. 'What goes on behind that cold, beautiful mask? Do you never think of anyone but yourself?'

His face was almost completely shadowed, his features seemed carved from some sombre metal. The only life came from his eyes. Under the hooded lids, they were like thin slashes of fire.

'Let go of me.' Kyla felt as if she would die from the pain in her heart. To lie under Adam—even an Adam devoured with bitterness and hate—called to mind the many times they had lain like this, herself in yielding ecstasy. When they had rolled over, her loosely pleated grey skirt had bunched up almost to her waist. Even though he showed no sign of being aware of it, one of his legs was bent, his knee thrusting between her thighs.

'You *will* be her matron of honour!'

Adam's hands moved from her shoulders to cup each side of her head as she tried to turn it away, to escape the anger in his eyes, and the aching familiarity of his breath.

'Do you hear me?' he persisted angrily when she didn't answer.

Kyla knew that if she didn't manage to escape she was going to burst out crying. The sobs were building in her chest, and she knew that she wouldn't be able to hold them back much longer.

'Yes, Adam. I——'

He didn't let her finish. With a groan that was so unexpected and heartfelt it made her throat ache with emotion, he pulled her against him, caressing her cold cheek tenderly with his roughly bristled jaw, holding her as if he never wanted to let her go. Shock scattered her senses as he slid his palms possessively over her full, high-thrusting breasts.

She felt as if someone was wringing out the blood from her heart. Never had she been so wrenched inside, her head screaming at her to break away, and every other cell in her body desperate to surrender to his erotic caress.

'No, no. . .' she pleaded, pushing her palms against his jaw as he kissed her eyelids, her hair, her throat. 'Adam, Adam, stop, you mustn't. . .'

The moss was soft, and because of the winds that had been scouring the land it was dry. The sky had become a luminous white, casting an unnatural light over everything—over Adam, picking out the silvered strands of his hair, making them shimmer like white frost.

'Hell, but I want you.' The longing in his voice sent a quiver through her body, and as if in protest her eyes closed. There was no mistaking the truth of Adam's admission; she almost moaned as she felt the insistent pressure through his cords against her silk-clad thigh. How easy it would be to give in. . .Sweet agony, to know he still desired her, to know he wasn't free to take her.

Kyla twisted her face against the thick wool collar of his jacket, and pressed trembling fingers against his temples.

'Oh, Adam,' she whispered, 'please let me go.'

She thought she was going to faint as, breath indrawn painfully, she waited for his response. Vaguely she was aware that Merle was whimpering close by, and that the world was still revolving, though moments before she had thought it had stopped on its axis.

Then slowly Adam's weight lifted from her, and in a moment his broad shoulders blotted out the light of the moon. In the near dark she saw his hand outstretched to help her up. He didn't say a word as he pulled her to her feet.

She bent her head to tie the buttons of her jacket. Oh, how weak she was. If Adam had persisted a moment longer, she couldn't have resisted him.

She heard his harsh breathing, heard his soft curse, a contemptuous sound. . .and she knew the contempt this time was for himself.

'It's all right, Adam.' Was that really her voice whispering into the space between them, gentling, reassuring? No one saw, she wanted to say. And there's no one else here at the loch-side in the moonlight to see us, standing together now, and not touching. 'I'll be matron of honour. Tell Nairne it's all right.'

She gave a little start as something wet and cold settled on her cheek. The first snowflake of winter. The air was clear and cold and very beautiful, and she inhaled deeply, as if trying to draw in strength for the moments ahead. Another snowflake fell, and yet another. Each one drifted down separately from the silver-streaked sky, touching the soft, pale skin of her cheeks like the quick, furtive kiss of a ghost. The ghost of the past. . .

Kissing her goodbye.

'It's snowing.' Adam turned his back to her and, though he appeared to be looking out over the loch, Kyla was sure he wasn't seeing the moon-dappled waves. His voice was muffled, but not so muffled that Kyla couldn't hear the bitter thread of unhappiness running through its husky timbre. 'Perhaps the roads will be bad tomorrow. Nairne and I are planning an engagement dinner at Redhillock. Rory Campbell will be there—he's to be my best man. You can come? I'll call for you around seven. Will Martha look after Kevin for a few hours?'

She stared at his dark figure outlined against the luminosity of the heavens, and felt her soul cry out with the agony of her emotions. Everything was so confused, so unpredictable. One moment Adam was sneering at her, the next kissing her with a desperate urgency, and now he was asking her with polite formality if she'd accept an invitation to dinner.

Kyla felt like a puppet as she nodded. 'Tomorrow night? Y. . .yes, I can make it. Once Kevin goes to bed in the evening, he doesn't stir till breakfast-time.' she was utterly amazed that she managed to sound so calm. Inside she felt as if she were falling apart at the seams!

Adam thrust his fingers through his long, dark hair, sweeping it from his forehead in a weary gesture as he turned to face her again. 'For Nairne's sake, we must be friends.' Kyla saw his hand reach out to her in a gesture of friendship, but his tone was impersonal as he went on, 'Agreed?'

Her own hand felt cold and stiff, but she forced it forward, watched as her fingers were clasped in his firm, warm grip. She was almost overwhelmed by a fierce surge of longing, longing for him to swing her into his arms, hold her tight, tell her it had all been a bad dream, that the past five years had never happened. . .

They were standing so close that if she swayed forward a few inches she could slip inside his open jacket, with her breasts pressed against his chest, her mouth touching the rough skin at his throat, her nostrils inhaling the male, earthy smell of him. . .

She closed her eyes to shut out the seductive, danger-ous thought. This man was engaged to her sister. He was as far out of her reach as he had been when she'd been married to Drew. Fate was determined to try her to the very limits of her endurance.

She didn't know which of them dropped their hand first. Or when it happened. It seemed to her afterwards that they had stood for an eternity, with messages best left unsaid passing between them by way of warm, clasping fingers.

But eventually they had broken away from each other.

As she stumbled alone along the avenue of beech trees leading to Glencraig House, she tried not to remember the way her body had reacted as she had lain beneath him. And she tried not to think about going to Redhil-lock Farm tomorrow night, about watching the man she loved make plans for his marriage to her sister.

Kyla's high-heeled boots clicked across the hallway of Glencraig House at five to seven on the following eve-ning. When she pushed open the kitchen door, she found Martha sitting dozing in front of the Raeburn stove with a copy of the *Sunday Post* scattered at her feet. Despite the nervous churning of her stomach, Kyla felt an amused smile twitch at her lips as she saw the packet of chewing gum on the housekeeper's lap. Martha, in her own way, was trying hard to quit smoking.

There was a startled grunt from the hunched figure in the rocking chair as Kyla gently touched her shoulder. 'Martha, I'll be going in a few minutes. Kevin's asleep. He shouldn't be any bother. Just check on him every fifteen minutes or so——'

'Landsakes, missy, are you going to another funeral?' Green eyes widened as they scanned Kyla's black wool dress and the black velvet bow she'd used to tie back her hair. 'I thought this was a party, to celebrate Nairne and Adam's engagement!' The wizened old face wrinkled into a knowing smile. 'Or maybe for you it's going to be more of a wake!'

There was no malice in Martha's words; there was rather an undertone of compassion. It brought a lump to Kyla's throat. She raised her hand and let her fingertips brush the soft black velvet confining her hair. 'It wouldn't be right for me to get all dressed up, so soon after Barclay's death, Martha.' She tried to sound reproving. 'I don't really have anything else that's suitable.'

The chair squeaked as Martha rocked back and forth rhythmically, her gnarled fingers gripping the wooden arms. 'You'll be meeting young Rory Campbell at Redhillock, then. He's all right. . .for a Lowlander, that is.' She leaned down and gathered the pages of the newspaper, tidying them and folding them neatly. 'So the laddie's sleeping. I just wish he'd come out of his wee boxie. When I saw that nice fall of snow, I thought he'd be raring to get out and play, but he just wanted to sit at the drawing-room window and look out.'

'He did have a walk, Martha. And had fun, I think, throwing snowballs into the loch. Remember, snow's no novelty to him. Toronto's been in the grip of winter for over a month, and more than a foot of snow lying over everything. I'm going into town tomorrow morning to see Alex Gordon. After that, I'll take Kevin to the stores and let him choose a new bike for Christmas. He had a tricycle, but we left it behind. I think he's ready for a real bike, with a set of training wheels. Is——'

'There's the front door bell.'

Martha, who had been slumped in her chair as if ready to fall asleep again, lurched up hastily, and the *Sunday Post* fell again to the floor. 'That'll be himself. I'll get it.'

'Why, Martha, is that a gleam I see in those green eyes? I have a suspicion that you have a soft spot for Adam Garvie!'

Kyla hardly knew what she was saying. Her nerves had been strung up all day, waiting for just this moment. Now that it had arrived, her senses scattered to the four winds; Martha was out of the kitchen and half-way to the front door before she herself had taken one step. She caught a sudden, distorted glimpse of herself in the gleaming chrome of the electric kettle on the countertop and paused abruptly, aghast at the pallor of her face. Her red lipstick seemed garish, emphasising the bright, nervous glitter of her eyes, and the tightly drawn skin over her cheekbones. I should have worn blusher, she thought. Martha's right, I do look as if I'm going to a funeral.

But she hadn't told Martha that she *had* considered wearing something more flattering. She had actually held another dress in front of her at the dressing-table mirror, a hot turquoise knit two-piece with a white Peter Pan collar; it clung in all the right places and made her look vibrant and alluring.

She had replaced it in the wardrobe with a sigh. Fine feathers, she had thought, not only make fine birds, but catch fine birds, and the last thing on her mind was to catch anyone. . .least of all Adam Garvie.

She had dreamed about him last night, and in the dream he had held her again, and she had believed he still loved her. When she awoke, it was to the sour realisation that though she and Adam were now committed, on the surface, to being friends, he didn't even like her. And, after what she had done to him, she would be surprised if he ever did come to like her again. But there was *something* between them. He wasn't indifferent to her. The tension between them last night made that quite clear. What had caused him to clasp her against him, kiss her so fervently? Was it just a lingering shred of the chemistry that had once drawn them together. . .or was it just plain lust, provoked by their closeness, her perfumed hair, the magic silvering of the moon?

She didn't know. But she *did* know that whatever it was, even if she dared to, she couldn't encourage it. She had lain awake wondering what would have happened if she'd surrendered to Adam's passionate embrace as they lay together on the moss. Her instincts told her that if she'd given in to her almost irresistible desire to return his kiss and feel her fingers weave through his crisp, unruly hair, there would have been no turning back for either of them. How would she have felt today, knowing she had made love with her sister's fiancé? How would Adam have felt? He couldn't hate her any more than he already did. . .but he would have hated himself, and the barrier between them would have been higher than ever. If he had been engaged to anyone else but Nairne, would she have decided to fight for the man she loved? She pushed aside the disturbing thought. His fiancée *was* Nairne, so the question didn't arise.

But she couldn't deny that there was something between them. Something that frightened her, it was so intense and so explosive. And *that* was why she had decided to wear the black dress; in it, she thought she looked drab, thin, asexual.

It wasn't what she wanted. But it was how it had to be.

There were only a couple of inches of snow lying on the road. Kyla knew she could easily have driven over to Redhillock herself, but she hadn't wanted to phone Adam and tell him. She hadn't wanted to initiate anything at all between them. It was easier just to go along with what they had planned the night before.

His car was an old Rover, not quite as smooth and luxurious as the Bentley, but it was comfortable, and had a pleasant smell of leather and perfume. . .the perfume that Nairne had been wearing the day before at Tigh Na Mara.

Before Kyla could wonder where they had been driving together. Adam answered her unformed question.

'Nairne's at Redhillock already. She's been there all afternoon, preparing dinner. I'm not sure what she's making, but it smells good.' They turned the corner at the end of the avenue of beech trees, and Adam paused while he shifted gears and picked up speed on the main road. 'Rory was pulling in in his old van as I left just now.'

Kyla tried to relax, but found it impossible. She had worn her fur coat over her dress and was far too warm in the heated car. Adam seemed quite comfortable in his sheepskin jacket. She had noticed as Martha ushered him into the hallway that he was wearing a royal blue sweater under it, with a pearl-grey shirt, and matching trousers. No wonder Martha had a gleam in her eye, Kyla thought wryly. A woman would need to be six feet under before being unimpressed by Adam Garvie!

She pulled off her black gloves and stuffed them into the deep pockets of her coat. 'Would you mind turning down the heat, Adam? It's awfully warm.'

From under her eyelashes she watched as his hand reached out to the panel and brushed the switch across.

'Sorry. I'd heard that North Americans were like hot-house plants and needed to be kept at a temperature of around ninety degrees.' He tossed her a sideways glance and Kyla felt her heart skip a beat as she saw a smile curl up the corner of his mouth. 'Didn't you get spoiled over there?'

Somehow, Kyla had been afraid that, when Adam had asked her the night before to be friends for Nairne's sake, he meant that they would be amicable only while in the presence of other people. Now it seemed as if he was going to be genuinely friendly to her, even when they were on their own.

'I guess I am spoiled a little,' she responded, trying to sound as calm as Adam. 'I'm fortunate that Barclay believed in keeping up-to-date with modern trends. Depending on coal fires as the sole source of heat is getting to be a thing of the past, isn't it?' she shifted sideways in her seat and for the first time looked at him openly. 'Have you modernised Redhillock, Adam?'

The drive from Glencraig House to the farm was short, and though Adam was driving carefully because of the slippy roads they were already approaching the narrow track leading to the farm. In the faint yellow light from the dashboard his face looked grim and uncommunicative, but when he spoke his tone was easy. 'You'll remember I was thinking about it five years ago when we planned to get married.'

Kyla felt the blood rush to her head as he spoke. So he wasn't going to skirt round the subject of their broken engagement—but the way he talked about it he might as well have been discussing the price of paint. There wasn't a trace of accusation in his tone, nothing to imply that he was now in any way upset by what had happened between them. Was this the best way to treat the past, to talk of it as if there had been no bitterness then, no grudges now? Kyla was sure it was, yet it was so difficult to accept Adam's glib assumption that for her it was no longer a painful subject.

She shook her head to clear her muddled thoughts. He'd asked her if she remembered what he'd planned to do with Redhillock. Of course she remembered. All the plans had included her, and they had made them together. They'd discussed where to put the heating units, what colour carpet to cover the living areas, what style furniture would suit their casual way of living. . .

'Yes, I remember.' Nervously, Kyla drew her gloves from her pockets and concentrated on smoothing the fine black suede over her fingertips. 'Did you go ahead and have it installed?'

She gasped as the car skidded. Adam had applied the brakes, and looking up, startled, she saw that he had parked the car parallel to a dark van at the side of the house, near the path leading to the front door.

As he turned the key in the ignition and switched off the headlights, they were thrown into darkness, a darkness that was soon filtered with the reflection of the snow. The sudden quietness in the car made Kyla painfully conscious of their closeness. Though they were at least a foot apart on the leather seats, the fact that they were confined in the warmth, their breath mingling as they faced each other, set her pulses racing.

'You'll see for yourself in a minute.'

For a moment, Kyla couldn't remember what they'd been speaking about. Her mind couldn't focus on anything but the bulk of his shoulders in his sheepskin jacket, the familiar shape of his head outlined against the faint light outside. Many, many times they'd sat like this when he'd switched off the car engine, but the silence between them had sizzled expectantly. Both had known that the cutting of the engine meant that they were going to reach for each other, she snuggling inside his jacket, he sliding his hands under her sweater, round her back, his touch sending splinters of sensation into her flesh. . .

'What. . .oh, yes.' She forced a smile. 'Yes, I guess I'm going to find out as soon as we go inside.' Her fingers tightened round her bag. 'You've probably done a lot in five years.'

She sat staring into space as Adam swung himself out of the car and came round to her side. When he opened her door, she was glad of his supporting hand at her elbow. She stumbled as she got out, but it wasn't because of the snow, it was because her legs were so weak that she thought they weren't going to support her.

As they walked in silence to the front door, she saw a shadow at the drawing-room window, thought she saw someone peep out from behind the corner of the curtain. Was it Nairne?

Kyla felt a shiver of apprehension skim down her spine as she contemplated the evening that lay ahead.

CHAPTER SIX

THE path had obviously been cleared out a short time before, but since then another layer of snow had fallen and it muffled the sound of their steps. Kyla was intensely aware of Adam's hand cupping her elbow, even through the thickness of her fur coat, and of the absent-minded way he was whistling 'White Christmas' under his breath. She was also intensely aware of the jauntiness of his walk, which gave the impression that all was right in his world.

Kyla could hardly believe that his attitude had changed so much. Of course, his nonchalant demeanour was just superficial, but it disorientated her. She felt as if she were in a dream and would waken at any minute to find herself back in her neat suburban house in Toronto.

A gust of wind shook the lamp hanging above the front door as they walked up the shallow steps.

'Watch, they're slippy——'

Adam's warning came too late. The red tiles beneath the thin layer of snow were treacherous underfoot, and Kyla felt the heel of her boot slip forward, throwing her off balance. With a startled gasp, she clutched automatically at Adam's jacket and, as she toppled backwards, she heard his explosive, 'Damn!'

The whole thing happened quickly, and was over in a second, but it left Kyla's heart thumping frantically. She let out a deep breath, and without even thinking flung a grateful smile up into Adam's face. He had an arm round her waist, the other grasping her roughly at the shoulder, so that they were embracing. Their bodies were clamped tightly together, and she felt helpless and feminine against his broad, muscular figure. A strand of her hair had worked its way loose from the velvet bow; now it blew across her lips, and she felt its silky texture against her teeth.

The near-accident had left her throat dry, and when she spoke, it was in a husky whisper. 'I. . .'

She found her voice trailing away as Adam reached to slide the errant strand from her cheeks, and her heart gave a painful lurch as she saw the expression in his grey eyes: a smoky, wounded expression that contrasted so strongly with his earlier blasé behaviour that it left her trembling.

She understood her own feelings only too well, but Adam's were a different matter. She had thought at first that the only thing he felt for her was hatred, yet several times since her return to Glencraig it had seemed that he'd been fighting some other emotion. . .one equally strong. Wasn't it only to be expected that the fierce passion he had felt for her before—the physical desire her body had aroused in him—would still exist despite his contempt for her behaviour? She knew that a man could desire a woman whom he neither loved nor respected, whereas for most women sex and love were inextricably intertwined. She had always been sensitive to other people's moods and emotions, and her instincts told her that Adam still wanted her physically. Was he finding it hard to control his desire?

He shook his head. 'Lord, but you're so beautiful. . .' His words were hoarse, and thick with emotion.

Kyla dropped her eyelids, not wanting him to see her pain. She felt his arms fall away, sensed that he moved from her, and then she heard him open the door. She kept her eyes closed, praying that when she opened them she'd find herself alone.

But she wasn't. Adam was standing in the open doorway, his face expressionless. 'Come on in, then, before you freeze the whole house.'

Kyla slipped past him, wondering how much more of this agonising turmoil she could take. As she shrugged her coat off her shoulders, she consoled herself with the thought that Adam had no idea that she was still in love with him. Tonight she would concentrate on reinforcing that belief, and then surely he'd put her out of his mind.

Adam took her coat, and as he put it on a hanger and hung it in the closet by the door she became aware of a delicious savoury aroma in the air. Something spicy was cooling, with onions, oregano, and who knew what else, and she felt her taste-buds spring to life.

'You were right, Adam, it certainly——'

'Adam's always right. That's one of his less endearing traits!'

Nairne must have been in the living-room, which was situated behind where Kyla was standing. Kyla felt herself freeze as she heard her sister's teasing chuckle. Was Nairne going to be like Adam, hiding her real feelings behind a friendly façade? And would this charade be easier to accept than outright hosility? Kyla's teeth nipped the soft inner flesh of her lower lip as she forced herself to turn round.

Nairne was crossing the wide hallway, the blue of her eyes intensified by the deep violet of her slim, ankle-length skirt, the toning shade of the long-sleeved blouse revealing her narrow waist and generous breasts. Though her mouth was curved in a welcoming smile, her eyes were wary.

'Kyla.' She held out her hands in welcome. 'I'm glad you're here. Adam told me how you ran into each other last night. Did you enjoy your walk along the loch-side?'

Kyla quickly tucked her handbag under her arm and took the cool, slender fingers in hers briefly, crushing back the longing to pull Nairne into her arms and give her a fierce hug. 'Yes, it was a beautiful evening, despite the cold wind. I've always loved strolling by the water.'

It wasn't till she was entering the drawing-room that

Kyla realised why she'd had a strong feeling of *déjà vu* when she'd come into the house, despite the fact that it was quite different from the way it had been five years before. Adam had carpeted the hallway, and furnished it exactly as they had planned together; now that she was in the drawing-room, she saw that he had done the same in here. The walls were painted white, the fitted carpet flowing from hallway into drawing-room a lovely soft green shade, and the chairs and sofas were attractively slip-covered in green and pink chintz. He had even hunted down the antique coffee-table and other pieces she'd admired in magazines. Bewilderment flooded her, even as she smiled at the very tall, sandy-haired man rising from his armchair by the fire. Why had Adam done it? Surely he would have wanted nothing around to remind him of her?

'Kyla, this is my boss—and our best man—Rory Campbell. He's from Edinburgh. . .but then, nobody's perfect!'

A firm, callused hand grasped Kyla's warmly. 'Don't mind Nairne. She heard Fanny Webster introduce me to someone with that line—in all seriousness—and hasn't missed a chance to use it since. I'm glad to meet you, Kyla.'

Rory reminded Kyla of an advertisement for porridge oats. Though he was dressed in a blue dress shirt, striped tie and grey flannels, she had immediately pictured him bare-chested and kilted, brawny legs apart, long hair blowing in a summer wind, as his strong arms tossed the caber at some Highland Games.

She smiled up into a pair of friendly brown eyes. 'It's nice to meet you too, Rory.' He wasn't as devastatingly handsome as Adam, she couldn't help thinking, but he was very good-looking, none the less. Dependable, safe, pleasant.

'Here, come and sit by me.' Still holding Kyla's hand, he pulled her down on to the sofa facing the fireplace. 'If we're to be partners at this wedding that's coming up, we should get to know each other. And were you as surprised as I was to find out that this pair was going to jump into marriage? Mind you, they've been knocking around forever, so far as I've heard. But sometimes these long-term relationships fizzle out——'

'No chance of that here.' Adam's cool voice broke into Rory's lively monologue. Kyla gently removed her hand from Rory's and looked up. Nairne and Adam were standing together, and Adam's arm was round Nairne's back, his fingers caressing her shoulder. 'We're set for the next hundred years, aren't we, love?' His eyes stared straight into Kyla's as he drew Nairne against his chest, and planted a tender, lingering kiss on her forehead.

The intimate gesture was so unexpected that Kyla had to bite back a gasp of dismay. Desperately she tried to conceal her stunned reaction. She felt as if Adam had stabbed her in the heart, and she was overwhelmed by an excruciatingly painful emotion—an emotion she had never felt before in her whole life. Yet, though it was completely alien to her nature, she had no difficulty whatsoever in recognising it. She could almost feel the edges of her heart curling green.

Jealousy.

When she and Adam had been engaged, he had always been extremely undemonstrative in public. Most of the time she hadn't minded, but once in a while she'd wished rather wistfully that he'd hold her hand, or touch her arm, in front of other people—to let them know he loved her, as she knew he loved her. But apparently it wasn't in his nature. When they were alone, he couldn't have been more loving or passionate. She had eventually come to realise that his intimate caresses were all the more valuable for being just between the two of them. Yet at one time she'd have given a great deal to be in the position that Nairne was in right now.

'What would you like to drink, Kyla?' Adam looked

down at her mockingly, and she slid her gaze away, only to find herself watching his hand weave through the cloud of hair at Nairne's nape. Was he doing it to distress her? Or was he touching Nairne because he couldn't keep his hands off her? Kyla tried to close her mind to her unhappy thoughts. Nairne and Adam were engaged. She must begin the formidable task of purging her heart of her love for him.

And how better to begin than by pretending to herself that she was looking for someone new?

'What are *you* drinking, Rory? If we're going to be partners, we should try to develop similar drinking habits!' She tucked the loose strand of hair behind her ear as, turning with an appealing smile to the man beside her, she glanced at his half-empty glass on the end table. 'Whisky?' She sank back against the comfortable cushions. 'Thanks, Adam. I'll have the same as Rory.'

For the first time that day she'd done something positive by deciding to flirt a little with Rory. It was harmless, and might even help ease the tension vibrating between herself and Adam and Nairne.

But when she glanced up and saw their expressions, her fingers tightened till her nails bit into her palms. What had she done now? Adam's face had darkened and his blue eyes sparked with anger. His hand was no longer at Nairne's neck. Instead his fingers were clenched into tight fists at his side, as if he were trying to control himself. Nairne's merry smile had disappeared, and a frown wrinkled her brow as if she were puzzled, but didn't quite know why.

The atmosphere had become more tense than ever. Kyla was vaguely aware that Rory was tapping the toe of his shoe against the leg of the coffee-table as she wondered what on earth she had said to cause their distress.

'Whisky it is.' Adam turned abruptly away, striding to the cocktail cabinet on the wall by the door, where the rigid set of his shoulders delivered their own unmistakable message. Hesitating for only a moment, Nairne smiled wanly and with a softly murmured, 'Excuse me for a minute while I see to the dinner,' she left the room, her light flat shoes soundless on the green carpet.

'Well, Kyla my girl, I don't know what you said, but——'

Rory's amused remark, delivered in a stage whisper, made Kyla jump. She swivelled round to look at him, feeling like a frightened rabbit. 'Wh. . .what?'

Warm brown eyes lost their jocularity as Rory's glance encompassed Kyla's face. She knew he was noting the pallor of her cheeks and the lines of strain around the mouth. Concern laced his voice as he said softly, 'Gosh, I'm sorry. . .Are you all right?'

Kyla managed a watery smile. Rory should have been a doctor, with his comforting bedside manner—though of course it would be very valuable in the social work he did. 'I'm fine. Really. It's——'

The strong smell of whisky snagged her attention. She looked up, and took the heavy crystal glass Adam was holding out to her. As she caught his eye, she felt her heart sink. Any pretence at friendship had disappeared. He was gazing at her with a contemptuous look that reminded her of the way he'd reacted when she returned his engagement ring five years ago.

Why?

Surely not because she had flirted with Rory Campbell?

'Is it going to be a big wedding, then, Nairne?' Rory paused with a forkful of lasagne half-way to his mouth. 'Hundreds of guest and——'

'Oh, no. Just a quiet family affair. Adam has no relatives in this part of the world and——'

She broke off with a rueful grimace and Kyla saw her exchange a smile with Adam. 'But that's not the real reason. I've never believed in grand, expensive weddings. There's so much money spent, so much attention given to arranging all the details that I've always felt that somewhere along the line, the real meaning of the ceremony gets lost.'

'Oh, I can't agree with you there!' Rory tilted his chair precariously as he leaned back with a teasing smile on his face. 'Surely it's just like a Christmas dinner—the turkey on its own would be delicious, of course, but without all the trimmings: the stuffing, gravy, brussels sprouts, carrots, bread sauce. . .I could go on and on!. . .wouldn't it lose some of its flavour?'

'Well, Rory Campbell, if you're going to be comparing me to a turkey——'

Rory's eyes glinted mischievously at the outraged expression on Nairne's face, but he turned his attention to Adam. 'And how about you, Adam, my good man? You don't believe in the trimmings, either?' He nodded meaningfully in the direction of Nairne's left hand which was toying with a fragment of bread roll on her side plate. 'You're not going to leave that slender hand bare till the wedding? Are you going to give your fiancée an engagement ring?'

'Nairne doesn't believe in elaborate weddings,' Adam said lazily, red wine glinting as he raised his glass to his lips, 'and I don't believe in engagement rings.' He spoke lightly, but Kyla watched with a tightening of her heartstrings as he reached for Nairne's hand. 'The ring that's important is the band of gold which I'll slip on this finger in June. As far as I'm concerned, an engagement ring is a meaningless bauble.'

Kyla felt a rush of heat suffuse her body as the full import of Adam's remark registered. He had tossed it off in a deliberately offhand manner, so that the casual listener wouldn't have given it a second thought. But she had learned since her return that nothing Adam said in her presence could be taken at face value, so she automatically dug below the surface for the underlying meaning.

She hadn't noticed before that the little dining-room with its Persian carpet and lovely old mahogany dining suite was so warm. Unable to face the narrowed challenge in his grey eyes, afraid he would interpret the hurt and pain she was trying to conceal, she let her glance slide to the electric fire with its glowing bars and realistic-looking logs, trying to ignore the trickle of perspiration running down her spine. There was no doubt in her mind that like herself he was remembering the day she'd returned the antique ruby ring—the ring which he'd then flung far into the heather.

When Rory interrupted her wretched thoughts with an offer to refill her wineglass, she nodded. 'Thanks, Rory. Yes, I'd love some more.'

She had never been a drinker, and her head was already spinning, what with the generous dram of whisky before dinner and the wine she had already consumed. But she felt so upset that she didn't care. Anything to dull the feelings that were cutting into her heart.

By the time they all returned to the living-room, she was glad of Rory's hand at her elbow. The room had tilted as she stood up, and her head was so light it felt as if it might just float away. It was a relief to sink down into the sofa—a relief that was short-lived, however, when Rory began talking shop-talk with his hostess, and Nairne said gaily, 'Let's not bore the others, Rory. Come and help me with the dishes while we discuss the problem, and kill two birds with one stone.'

Adam opened his mouth immediately to protest, and Kyla leaned back helplessly against the cushions as they airily waved aside his objections. He glared as Rory strode out behind Nairne, closing the door firmly behind them.

In the awkward silence that followed their departure, Kyla didn't know where to look. Adam stood for a moment, fists clenched aggressively, and then, without letting his eyes fall on her, he stalked to the fireplace where he stood with one elbow on the mantelpiece while he gazed into the fire. Kyla could see only his profile, harshly outlined against the white-painted wall, and it seemed strained and grim. How he must hate her, Kyla thought, that he couldn't bear to share a few minutes alone with her.

For the first time since her return, it struck her with terrible force that she might have been unspeakably selfish in coming back. It seemed now that Martha had been right when she had forecast that Kyla's arrival in Glencraig would create a storm.

When she had made her plans, the only person she'd been concerned about was Kevin. She hadn't considered how her reappearance might tear anew at Adam, and at Nairne. It had, however; and now she could see that it hadn't been fair to sweep back into their orderly lives, wreaking havoc with emotions which after an interval of five years must surely have stabilised.

Adam had promised that they would all try to be friends, but she could see already that it was going to be an uphill battle. Adam and Nairne were the ones who had been wronged; it would be up to Kyla herself to pour oil on the troubled waters. If she succeeded, however, her sacrifice would be worth it.

'Adam?' Her voice was tentative. 'We haven't talked much about the plans for the wedding. Would you like to tell me——'

He thrust his muscular figure away from the mantelpiece and confronted her, his hands in the pockets of his pearl-grey slacks in a manner that was uniquely masculine and uniquely his. His eyes were still angry, his mouth set in a thin line.

'Why, of course, Kyla. What do you want to know?' He stepped forward so that he was towering over her, and, despite her feeling of apprehension as she saw the sarcastic twist of his mouth, she couldn't help noticing what a stunning contrast his royal blue sweater made to his black, silver-threaded hair. She even wondered distractedly why Nairne hadn't told him it was time he had his hair cut; it curled a little above his ears, and into the crisp grey collar of his open-necked shirt. She almost jumped as his voice rasped on, 'The wedding will be held in the parish kirk, of course, with the reception here, at Redhillock. Nairne wants to do the catering herself, except for the actual cake, which she'll order from Albert the Baker's.'

He began talking in a low, intense tone, reeling off more information as if by rote. 'It'll be a late afternoon affair, with a buffet dinner here. We'll clear the large sitting-room at the back for dancing. As for the honeymoon, our destination's going to be a secret. . .even from Nairne. . .till we're well on our way. I've just told her to pack summer dresses and a bikini and lots of suntan lotion.' He took one hand out of his pocket and impatiently swept his hair from his forehead. 'She's going to make her own wedding dress—lace, I think, with a long train. And oh, one last thing——'

Kyla felt a shiver of apprehension ripple through her as she saw an unmistakable flicker of malice in his blue eyes. What was he going to say now? Obviously something that he knew was going to hurt her. And she could just tell he was milking the moment, making her wait. She inhaled a deep, calming breath. She was ready for it, whatever it was.

Adam's eyes were an opaque blue-grey, like the sky before a storm, and his hair had fallen over his forehead again giving him a deceptively vulnerable, boyish look that contrasted with the anger apparent in every other aspect of his bearing. Kyla almost winced as his voice grated roughly in her ears. 'You'll be most anxious to know. Her dress is to be pure white. Unlike her sister,

Nairne will still be a virgin when she comes to the marriage bed.'

Kyla thought she had prepared herself for anything he could say, but she had been mistaken. As her horrified gasp filled the space between them, Adam pivoted on his heel and strode to the cocktail cabinet.

She was on her feet before she could stop herself, her temper completely out of control as she stormed after him. 'Adam Garvie, you are *despicable*! The rudest, cruellest, most unfair——'

He turned round just in time to receive the full force of her palm against his cheek. Kyla thought she could hear the wild drumming of her own heart as she confronted him, her hands on her hips, her eyes blazing with outrage. 'You have gone too far this time, you. . .you *bastard*!'

Adam stared at her as if he couldn't believe what had just happened. Slowly, as if in a dream, he raised one hand to touch his cheek, where already through the red mist of anger Kyla could see her fingerprints. He blinked incredulously as he stared down at her.

His voice was thick and ominous. 'That hurt, you little——'

His arms snaked out and he gripped her wrists with ruthless fingers, twisting her arms behind her back. 'What the hell was that for?'

Kyla tried to control her fast, rough breathing, but it was impossible. Her breasts heaved up and down beneath her black wool dress, her knees felt so weak, she hoped she wasn't going to keel right over. She lifted a furious face to him and cried, 'You know damn well what that slap was for, Adam. Apart from the fact that you were way out of line, discussing Nairne so intimately with anyone, even me, you had no right to. . .to. . .'

'To what? Remind you that you were second-hand goods by the time you married Drew Ferguson? Did he know that,' he jeered, 'or did you manage to fool the poor man into thinking he was the first?' With a savage wrench of her arms that she thought might twist them out of their sockets, he pushed her away from him. 'Just like you fooled me?'

Kyla staggered backwards as if he had hit her. Oh, how could he? Even as she reeled from the horror of his accusation, she involuntarily recalled the first time they'd made love, the beauty of it, the magic of it, made all the more perfect because there was no doubt that Adam had been the first. . .

How could he tarnish that memory? Was there no end to his viciousness?

Kyla felt her shoulders slump in defeat. She couldn't fight someone who used such dirty tactics. There was a limit to her endurance, after all. Forcing one foot to follow the other, she walked over to the sofa, fighting back a feeling of nausea. What a mistake she'd made in coming back. Her return had flung them all back into the past, and reopened all the old wounds.

She couldn't stay.

As soon as the thought entered her mind, she was flooded with despair, but also with certainty that it was undeniably true.

Plans swirled round and round in her head as she sank back into her seat, closing her mind to Adam's presence. She'd go and see Alex Gordon tomorrow as planned, tell him to do everything he thought best, and she'd sign everything right away. Then she'd leave, before she did any more damage to herself and everyone else.

Kevin. . .Poor Kevin. But there would be no happiness for him here either, if things were to go on this way. She would take him to——

The shrill ringing of the telephone on one of the side tables cut into the chaos of her mind. She turned in the direction of the sound as Adam picked the handset up on the second ring. He had his back to her as he said curtly, 'Garvie here.'

Kyla got up unsteadily. She'd go to the bathroom and compose herself before the others returned from the kitchen. As she slipped the strap of her bag over her shoulder, she heard Adam say sharply, 'What's wrong, Martha?'

The dizziness left Kyla's head in one split second, and all she could think of was Kevin. One moment she was at the sofa, the next she was tugging wildly at Adam's sleeve. 'Adam, what is it? Kevin?'

'I'll have her home right away. Hang on, Martha.'

Kyla clung to Adam's jacket as if it were a lifeline. 'What is it?' Her voice was high and thready. 'Is he hurt?'

'Calm down, Kyla.' Adam put the phone down and said, 'He's all right. But he's had a bad nightmare, and Martha can't get him to settle down——'

'Is he hysterical? Tell me, damn you, tell me what she said!'

Kyla was at the door as she spoke, running across the hall and pulling her coat from the closet. As she tried to open the front door, Adam clamped his hand over hers. 'Just a minute, don't panic. *He's all right.*' He shouted in the direction of the kitchen at the back of the house, 'Nairne?'

Immediately a door opened and a laughing, flushed Nairne appeared. 'Yes, what is it? Oh, you're not leaving already——?'

'I'm driving Kyla home, Nairne.' Adam grabbed his sheepskin jacket from the closet and shrugged it on. 'Kevin's had a nightmare. I'll be back as soon as I can.'

'Thank you for a lovely dinner—I'm so sorry for spoiling your party.' Kyla paused briefly in the doorway.

Nairne hurried across the hallway, and even in Kyla's distress she could see the genuine concern on her sister's face. 'Oh, the poor lamb. Phone me as soon as he gets settled. Perhaps if it's not too late, you'll come back?'

A sob caught in Kyla's throat as she stumbled through

the doorway, hardly hearing Adam's, 'Take care. Don't slip again.' The last thing Kyla saw as she hurried through the doorway was Nairne's troubled face, the last thing she heard was her, 'I do hope he's all right. Let us know. . .'

Don't over-react, Kyla said to herself over and over as Adam pressed his foot to the accelerator. He's had these nightmares before, they always pass.

'Don't worry. He'll be just fine.' Adam's profile was grim, though his voice was reassuring. 'I'm sure he'll be sound asleep by the time we get there.'

'No, no, he won't.' Kyla tried to keep her voice steady, but it wavered as she fought back the apprehensive tears. 'He's had them before, they go on all night. It takes hours for him to settle down.'

As they turned into the beech-lined driveway, Adam said huskily, 'Kyla, I'm sorry. What I said before, there was no excuse for it. It was wrong of me. Forgive——?'

'There's nothing to forgive.' In her distress, Kyla didn't even bother to look at Adam. All her attention was focused on the lights of Glencraig House ahead. 'It's all my own fault. I made a mistake in coming back. You won't have to worry any more about trying to be friends with someone you hate and despise. I've decided to go away. Back to Toronto.'

As she finished, Adam brought the Rover to a screeching halt. 'Kyla, no! You——'

'Thanks for the drive. Adam. Goodnight.'

She didn't wait to hear what he had to say. She slammed the car door behind her and ran into the house, her blood chilling as she ran up the stairs and heard Kevin's hysterical sobs, his shrill voice screaming, 'I want my daddy! I want my daddy!'

The first thing she saw when she flew into the bedroom was Kevin's thin little body, rigid as a board, fighting against Martha's restraining arms. In the pink glow from the bedside-lamp, the housekeeper's face looked flushed, her green eyes bright.

'Oh, Martha, I'm sorry. I'd never have left if I'd thought this would happen.'

The stooped figure gave her charge's damp, rumpled hair a soothing caress as she got up from the bed. 'Don't worry, lass, I've brought up ten of my own. I'll go down and put on the kettle. You'll be needing a strong cup of tea when you get him settled.'

Kevin had halted his screams when he heard his mother's voice, but as the door closed behind Martha he began wailing. 'I want my daddy. . .'

Kyla's coat slid to the floor as she threw it down at the end of the bed. 'Hush, darling, Mummy's here now. You just had a bad dream. It's all over. . .'

His cheeks were wet with tears as she pulled him into the curve of her body and pressed kisses on his thin, bony face. 'Don't cry any more, you'll only get more upset. Here, put your head on my shoulder and close your eyes.'

She gasped as he twisted away from her and flung himself face down on the pillow, his little back heaving as he sobbed uncontrollably. 'No, no, I want my *daddy*. . .'

Gulping back her own sobs, Kyla reached for the narrow shoulders, the hands that were gripping the pillow. 'How about a nice——?'

'Kyla? Is there anything I can do to help?'

Kyla's heart lurched as she heard the male voice just behind her. For one mindless moment, she thought it was Drew, suddenly, amazingly, come back to life. But when she swivelled round she saw Adam looming over her, a deep frown lining his brow.

Stunned, Kyla just stared at him, hardly noticing that Kevin's screaming had stopped. In the frozen moment, she heard a rustle beside her and, twisting abruptly, she realised that Kevin was sitting up, rubbing his eyes, staring at Adam in just the way she herself had been staring at him a second before.

'Bad dreams, huh?' Adam moved around Kyla and hunkered down so that he was on eye level with Kevin. 'I used to have those when I was about your age.' He reached out and with the pad of one thumb, carefully brushed away a tear that clung like a seed pearl to Kevin's lower lashes. 'I'd wake up so scared, and so wanting to be hugged. . .but somehow even that didn't help.'

Kyla felt her heart swell with emotion as she watched Adam with Kevin. Her son's gaze, grave and glistening, clung to Adam's eyes, just as he himself appeared to be clinging to his every word. The sound of his erratic, hiccuping sobs punctuated Adam's low, soothing words.

'I finally found out that there was only one thing that chased away the bad dream.' Adam chuckled. 'Would you like me to tell you what it was?'

Kevin's head moved up and down in a nod, and he whispered huskily, 'Yes, please.'

Adam's hands were gentle as he cupped the little head between his palms and, bending close, murmured something in his ear that Kyla couldn't hear. Whatever it was, it made Kevin's lips turn up at the corners in a wavering smile.

His eyes flickered over to Kyla. 'Can he, Mom?'

It was incredible. She had never been able to soothe him so quickly. Usually she had to fight his unwillingness to give in to her soothing, many a time she was still trying to calm him when dawn broke. Yet Adam, with a few words, had quietened him with apparent ease.

'Can he what, sweetheart?' She touched his cheek with her fingertip. 'I didn't hear. . .'

Her gaze moved to Adam's face and his expression was so intense, she had to swallow a lump in her throat. Now that the emergency was over, she was suddenly aware of the situation. She and Adam in the child's bedroom, quieting him after a nightmare. Just like a family. It was obvious Kevin and Adam got along; it was breaking her heart just to watch them.

Adam's low voice broke into her thoughts. 'I told him that when I had nightmares, my dad used to sleep with me, and promise to fight them off for the rest of the night. It always worked.' His mouth quirked in a lop-sided smile. 'I've promised Kevin I'll stand in for his dad, if he'll let me, and lie here with him till he drops off.' He raised his eyebrows as he heard the hiss of Kyla's indrawn breath. 'OK with you?'

She exhaled after she thought she must have held her breath for an eternity. Adam sleep here, with Kevin? Oh, what a muddle. Just when she'd decided to leave, Kevin, for the first time in a year, was showing signs of becoming attached to someone. Why, oh, why did that someone have to be Adam?

'All right, sweetheart.' She looked at Kevin as she spoke, and he gave a relieved, hiccuping sigh. Falling back on to his pillow, he curled his hands into Adam's.

'Take off my shoes, Kyla? As you can see, my hands are occupied, and I don't want to mark this lovely quilt. . .'

'Adam Garvie!'

Kyla bit her lip to hide an involuntary smile. As she knelt on the carpeted floor and untied Adam's shoes, she was struck with an almost irresistible desire to slide her fingers under the cuff of his trousers, and follow the contours of his muscled calves.

A desire that she squashed immediately as a picture of Nairne's anxious face flashed into her mind. With a 'There, that's it!' she got to her feet, and stood back as Adam swung his legs on to the bed. For a moment she paused, not quite knowing what to do.

'Kiss me goodnight, Mom.'

Kevin's bed was narrow, and it was right against the wall. He was snuggled up at the far side from Kyla, and she had to lean over Adam to reach the little face turned up to her like a pale pink flower. She felt her nerves quiver as her breasts brushed Adam's shoulder, forced herself not to look at his face to see his reaction.

'Goodnight, sweetheart. Don't forget, we're going shopping for that new bike tomorrow. Think about it as you drop off to sleep. . .'

'Now Adam's turn.'

'Wh. . .what?'

'A goodnight kiss for Adam, Mom. So he can sleep, too.'

Automatically Kyla's eyes, wide with dismay, turned to Adam. They locked glances, and Kyla was intensely aware of the involuntary hiccuping sobs that were still coming from Kevin.

'Hurry up, Mom.'

Kyla placed her palms on the edge of the bed to support herself as she leaned over. Adam wouldn't let her eyes slide away, he was drawing her down, drawing her into his sphere of magnetism. Finally, at the very last minute, she let her eyelashes drop, closing out the smoky, glazed look that was sending dangerous, frightening sensations spiralling through her.

Their lips touched, hers warm, trembling, his firm, full, tasting of wine and coffee. It was a passionless kiss—it really wasn't a kiss at all. It was sweet, and it was innocent, just like the kiss she'd just given Kevin.

Kyla raised her face and looked down at Adam. He was lying with his eyes shut, his face pale. Forbidden, she thought despairingly. I love him and he's forbidden to me.

She fought back a moan as she whispered, 'Goodnight,' and with one final glance at Kevin, his head angled in the curve of Adam's arm, she scooped up her coat from the floor, and stumbled from the room.

CHAPTER SEVEN

'Kyla. . .Kyla. . .wake up.'

Kyla heard someone murmuring her name, the sound spiralling softly round and round in her head. For a confused moment she wondered if she was dreaming, but when she opened her eyes and looked up she saw Adam. He was leaning over her, his grey eyes wary.

Feeling completely disorientated, she threw a quick glance around, and when she saw that she was in the kitchen everything came rushing back to her. She had come downstairs and phoned Redhillock; then, after having a cup of tea with Martha, she had sent the exhausted housekeeper off to bed, and she herself had curled up in the old kitchen rocker. Lulled by the heat from the stove and content in the knowledge that Kevin was safe with Adam, she must have drifted off to sleep.

'What time is it?' She stifled a yawn. Her legs were tucked up under her, and with an inconspicuous fluid motion she smoothed the skirt of her black dress down over her bared knees. Prompted by the movement, the chair started rocking gently. 'Is Kevin. . .?'

'He's sound as a top.' Adam looked at his watch. 'Good heavens, it's almost midnight!' His glance followed Kyla's hand as she reached to the table beside her for the velvet ribbon she'd removed from her hair earlier. 'I didn't mean to doze off—Nairne and Rory, they're going to be——'

'Don't worry, Adam.' Kyla laid the ribbon on her lap and gathered the heavy silk rope of her hair to one side. Dividing it into three sections, she hoped Adam wouldn't notice her fingers were trembling as she began plaiting it in front of her right shoulder. 'As soon as I came downstairs I called Redhillock. I told Nairne that Kevin had corralled you and that you might be a while getting home.' She had managed to speak calmly on the phone, but her heartbeats had been skittering just as wildly then as they were now. 'Nairne said that they would wait till around ten, and if you hadn't come back Rory would drive her to Tigh Na Mara.'

Eyes downcast, she finished her braiding, and twined the curl at the end of her hair around her index finger. Finally she secured it with the ribbon, and couldn't delay any longer the moment she'd have to look up at Adam. The rocker creaked as she unwound herself and got to her feet.

She forced her lips into a grateful smile. 'I really appreciate your coming home with me and helping with Kevin. I've never seen him settle so quickly before. It was nothing short of miraculous the way you handled him.'

Adam's face was grave. 'He's a bonny little lad. Drew must have been proud of him.'

Kyla tried to look away. It was painful for her, being so close to him. She felt caught up in the strength of his male magnetism, a strength of which he seemed totally unaware. It drew her, and it bound her, as it always had in the past.

She stepped around him, and stood by the table, with her back pressed against it. 'Yes, Drew was awfully proud of him, Adam. We both were.'

She saw his jaw tighten before he turned away. 'Can I have a drink?'

'Oh. . .sorry. . .of course. What would you like?' Kyla reached into a cupboard behind her and found a glass. 'I know Martha has a bottle of whisky right here in the kitchen—for medicinal purposes, she insists! Ah, here it is. Will a dram of the best Ferguson do?'

Adam's brows were knitted together. 'Och, anything,' he said impatiently.

He began pacing up and down the long kitchen, his hands in his pockets. Kyla bit her lip. Why hadn't he just left! She had the feeling that he was building up to talk about something important. Surely he wasn't going to choose this moment to rake up the past? With a tired sigh, she reached into the cupboard for a second glass—Dutch courage was what she needed.

As the amber liquid gurgled from the bottle, she saw out of the corner of her eye that Adam had come to a halt at the window, and was looking out into the darkness. What was he seeing? she wondered. 'Do you want ice, or maybe some water in it?'

He swivelled round and with a curt shake of his head resumed his pacing. 'Nothing.'

Kyla laid his drink on the table and walked to the sink, where she splashed a generous amount of cold water into her own glass. When she turned round, Adam had taken up his stance in front of the stove and was gulping down his dram as if he were dying of thirst after weeks in the desert.

Hesitantly she moved to the far side of the table so that she was facing him, and sat down. She lifted her own glass, not because she was in any hurry to drink, but rather to occupy her hands.

Adam was staring at her. Disconcerted, she sipped at the whisky, grimacing as its harshness bit at the back of her throat just as the harshness of his voice grated in her ears. 'I want to talk to you.'

She watched from under her long eyelashes as he shoved his empty glass to the side. The mouthful of whisky that she'd swallowed had curled hotly to the pit of her stomach, and now she raised her glass to her lips and sucked in some more. Immediately, she felt it streaming through her veins, running up her arms, rising to her brain and making it foggy.

'About what?'

Her words seemed to echo inside her head, and she

wasn't sure if he had heard her or not. His eyes had never left her and they were completely expressionless. They made her nervous. Swallowing the lump in her throat, she lifted the glass to her lips and drained the remaining whisky. She felt as if she were on fire from the stomach up; if she lit a match in front of her mouth and exhaled she just might go up in flames.

Adam's hair had fallen over his forehead, shadowing the tired lines around his eyes, but his features were pinched, his expression haggard. 'I'm sorry about what I said earlier.' The words of apology were slowly spoken, almost painfully dragged out, as if he found it difficult to express himself. 'You had every right to slap me——'

'Oh, no, Adam!' Kyla pushed her chair away and stood up. 'There was no excuse for that. I'm deeply ashamed of my behaviour. I had time to think about it after I came downstairs. When I told Martha how good you were with Kevin, she told me how. . .how bitter you were. . .' Kyla couldn't believe she was saying what she was. But now that she'd started she had to finish. 'She told me how bitter and moody you were for a long time after I left Glencraig. How. . .heartbroken. Adam, will you ever forgive me? Am I asking too much?'

She longed with all her heart to reach out and touch his arm; perhaps that way she'd be able to convey all the regret she felt for the way she'd hurt him, but she knew she shouldn't. He wasn't hers to touch. Not any more. Not ever again.

The royal blue of his sweater darkened his eyes till they were almost as black as his pupils. 'Martha was right. There was no secret about it. I really went off the deep end. It knocked me for six when you took off with Drew. But I've learned to live with what happened.' His voice was even and tightly controlled. 'You were only twenty-one. It was selfish of me to think that just because I felt so strongly about you that you felt the same as I did—that money wasn't important, that if we loved each other enough, we could make it. Not all people have the same values.'

Kyla stood with her expression frozen as he reached for the whisky bottle and gripped it by the neck.

'More?'

When she shook her head, he filled his glass again and thumped the bottle down on the table. Nursing the glass in one hand, he went on woodenly, 'I despised you for a long time. I don't mind admitting that. Now I'm not so judgemental. I think you're one of the strong ones: you see what you want and you go after it, no matter who you hurt. There's not much romance in that approach to life, but——' he moved his broad shoulders in a careless shrug '—if that's the way you are, then you can't help it. You obviously had a good marriage with Drew, and together you produced a fine son.' He paused while he tilted his glass to his mouth and swallowed. 'No, Kyla, you looked out for Number One, and I'm not blaming you for that any more. I just thank heaven that Nairne's going to be happy at last.'

Kyla desperately wished she'd taken him up on his offer of a second drink. Though her senses had been numbed slightly by the whisky she'd consumed, Adam's speech had jolted her into instant sobriety. She stepped back a little and found her hands gripping the edge of the table.

'You didn't mean what you said in the car, did you, Kyla?'

Kyla tried to sort out the chaos in her brain. What had she said in the car? Had she spoken to him at all? She had been so worried about Kevin. . .

She shook her head confusedly. 'What did I say?'

'You said you'd changed your mind. Said you were leaving and going back to Canada.' His voice was low, intense. 'Did you mean it?'

Oh, yes, she had meant it. At the time. But when she thought of the way Kevin had begun responding to

Adam, she was torn. How could she leave now, when Kevin was beginning to show the first signs of being ready to trust again?

'You *did* mean it! Your very silence speaks for itself.'

Kyla started as Adam's savage oath grated in her ears.

'You can't go hauling your son back and forth across the globe! He needs stability, family—all the things you told me about when we spoke at Barclay's funeral.' Adam raked his dishevelled hair back off his face. 'I *know* you're worried about——'

'Yes, I told you my reason for coming back to Glencraig, Adam. It *was* for Kevin's sake. I hoped— well, I told you what I hoped—that we would fit into a happy family atmosphere, and that he'd come out of his shell and be happy like he used to be. But that would only work if we stopped all this fighting. You and I. . .we. . .we've done nothing but shout at each other. . .and. . .tonight. . .tonight. . .'

'Dammit to hell, Kyla, I'm not a monster! Do you think I'm inhuman? I swear it won't happen again. We can both make the effort. . .'

Kyla sighed. 'I'm not going to argue with you. Of course, you're right. Kevin likes you and responds to you. He hasn't been like that with anyone since Drew died. So even if I wanted to go now, I couldn't. But you're a busy man. Do you have time to be a. . .I was going to say a father-figure, for Kevin, but it really should be an uncle-figure, shouldn't it, as he's going to be your nephew soon. . .do you have time to be there for Kevin, at least till he learns to cope with his loss?'

Adam laid his half-empty glass on the table. For the first time since he'd wakened her from her dreamless sleep in the rocker, she saw his face relax a litle. 'I'll be glad to.'

Kyla felt as if her mind was split into two parts. The first was concentrating on his promise to help, and she was conscious that he had lightened the load of her burden with his generous offer to share it. But the other part of her mind was still reeling in protest from his harsh accusation that when she'd jilted him she'd been looking out for Number One. How wrong he was! If she *had* looked out for Number One five years ago, as he believed, she'd be happily married to him right now, and they might have had a son Kevin's age—perhaps even a daughter as well. . .

'I'd best be going, then, now that we've got that settled.' Adam put his glass into the sink and turned towards the doorway.

All of a sudden, tiredness spread through Kyla's body like a debilitating drug. She felt her legs drag as she followed him from the kitchen through to the front hall, and she leaned against the wall as he thrust his arms into his sheepskin jacket.

His eyes were narrowed as they raked her face and listless figure. 'You're needing a good night's sleep. You're going to see Alex Gordon in the morning, aren't you?'

'Yes, ten o'clock,' she returned automatically.

Tightening his mouth into a grim line, he snapped, 'Watch yourself with that old lecher. Rich widows are right up his street. . .'

After Kyla locked the front door behind Adam, she leaned against it for a long time, the smooth oak cool against her burning forehead. Of course, she was delighted that Kevin had taken to Adam, and that she herself was once again on speaking terms with Nairne. But, though she was hopeful now that her dream of a warm family atmosphere for Kevin might eventually be realised, she couldn't ignore the wave of depression that surged over her, almost swamping her.

She was caught in a tenuous trap.

Of all the people for Kevin to turn to, why did it have to be Adam? He had promised he'd be there for Kevin and, knowing Adam, his word was his bond. So, for as long as Kevin needed Adam's presence, Adam would be very much a part of their life.

It was going to rip her apart, seeing him and Nairne together as man and wife, knowing they were sleeping together, waking up in each other's arms in the morning, sharing the wonder of their love. . .

Feeling as if the point of a knife was twisting round and round in her heart, she pushed herself away from the door and trudged slowly up the winding staircase. How wrong she had been in believing that her problems would be over if she and Kevin were accepted by the family and friends she loved.

On the contrary, her problems were just beginning.

'No, thank you, Alex. I won't stay for coffee.' Kyla rose gracefully from her chair in Alexander Gordon's handsomely furnished office and lifted her burgundy jacket from where she'd earlier slung it over a leather sofa. 'Kevin and I are going shopping for a bike this morning.' She turned her attention to her son, curled up in an armchair with Polar, his white stuffed bear. 'And he's been so good, I don't want to keep him waiting. Are you ready, sweetheart?'

A strong smell of hair lotion permeated the air as the lawyer came round to the front of his desk. Kyla was aware that his eyes were watching her every move as she slipped on her coat, and then zipped up Kevin's snowjacket. Thank goodness Barclay's will *was* straightforward, as he'd said at the funeral, and that Alex had everything under control.

'The big decision, my dear, will be whether to keep on the distillery, with Garvie managing it, or to put it up for sale. As I said before, the whisky business isn't what it used to be.' He smiled his oily smile. 'Things have changed indeed.' One manicured hand reached out to pat Kevin on the head condescendingly. 'Lucky man, getting a new bike. When I was your age, my boy, the war was on. Children were lucky to have bikes at all. I remember mine; it was what they called "utility". . .like most of the other goods that were available. . .Well, no good reminiscing! Time marches on!

'Think about what I've suggested, Kyla, and get back to me in a week or two. You'll want to have a long talk with Garvie, of course. He knows more about the state of Ferguson Whisky than I do. I'll set up an appointment for you to see him——'

'Heavens, no, Alex. I can manage that by myself.' What on earth did he think she was, a Barbie doll? 'I'll be talking to Adam—probably later today.' She laid her hand on Kevin's shoulder. 'Thanks again, Alex—and for the offer of coffee. Sorry we haven't time. I'll be in touch.'

As her boots clattered down the wooden stairs, echoed by the lighter sound of Kevin's, she breathed a sigh of relief. Thank goodness that was over. She had a lot to think about, of course, but she'd do that later. Right now she would concentrate on Kevin, make sure he enjoyed his outing.

As they stepped out on to the pavement, she paused for a moment. It was a beautiful, bright morning, with the sun shining on the snow-shrouded town, making it glisten as if someone had scattered a confetti-like shower of diamonds over everything. The air was clear and crisp and frosty, and it made Kyla's heart sing.

'Morning, Kyla.'

'Good morning, Mrs Webster.' Kyla raised a hand in greeting as Fanny Webster's shrill voice yodelled across from the other side of the narrow street. 'Lovely day!'

She bent down to pull on Kevin's hood, and tuck his fingers into his mittens. 'Shall I carry Polar?'

'I can do it myself.'

'I can do it myself, *thank you*.' She tweaked his nose teasingly.

'I can do it myself, thank you,' he repeated automatically.

'Now,' Kyla said, biting her lip as she scanned the stores to her right and left, 'I know there used to be a bike shop somewhere near here. It was called. . .oh, dash, I can't even remember what it was called. Dozzi's? Cozzi's?'

'Pozzi's!'

Kyla jumped as a voice teased her from behind. She whirled round and felt her breath catch in her throat. 'Nairne! Where did you come from? I've been looking up and down the street for the bike shop. . .*Pozzi's*. . .and I didn't see you?'

Nairne chuckled. 'I was in my office.' Her hair shone like a flaming bush as she tossed her head back to the building Kyla had just left. 'Rory and I work in the ground floor of Alex Gordon's building.'

As Nairne bent down and said to Kevin, 'I hear you had company in bed with you last night,' Kyla's gaze encompassed her sister's smart emerald-green coat with brass buttons, her high-heeled tan leather boots. She looked like a model with her slender figure and unusual, vibrant colouring. And every other person who passed seemed to call, 'Aye there, Nairne,' or 'Good morning, Nairne.'

'What have you got there, Kevin? Are you going to let your Auntie Nairne see?'

Despite the gentle coaxing tone, Kevin wouldn't raise his head or answer. He stood with his little mittened hands clutching his bear, his eyes fixed on the snow at his feet, his body pressed against Kyla's legs.

She grimaced apologetically to Nairne. 'Sorry,' she murmured softly. 'He'll come around. Adam was awfully good with him last night. He told you about it? It was too bad we spoiled your party——'

'Never mind. Though we didn't get to talk about the wedding! You will be matron of honour, won't you?'

For the first time since her return, Kyla looked into her sister's blue eyes and saw a hint of the old Nairne. The look was tentative, wary, but it was no longer hostile.

'Of course I will. I'm honoured that you asked me.' Kyla's voice was husky with emotion. 'I——'

'Well, what's going on here?'

Without turning round, Kyla knew that it was Adam. She felt her heart jump in her chest, felt as if her smile was pasted on, as she turned with an appearance of casualness.

Adam must have been walking down the street behind her. Now he embraced Nairne lightly and brushed a kiss on her forehead. 'Is it a gathering of the Drummond clan, or can anyone join in?'

Nairne flashed him a smile. 'Well, just this once, but we won't make a habit of it. We Drummonds are fussy about who we're seen with!'

Adam laughed and, with a quick 'Good morning' to Kyla, turned his attention to Kevin. 'Hello, there. Have you bought your new bike yet?'

Adam had casually draped an arm round Nairne's shoulder, his dark good looks set off by the charcoal-grey duffel coat he was wearing over black cords and a heavy white crew-neck sweater. What a perfect couple they made. Kyla had to look away as again, just as it had the night before when she had watched Adam kiss Nairne, jealousy tore at her. She wondered if she had ever in her life felt more miserable. Her heart was breaking. . .but her mind was struggling to accept the humiliating fact that she was jealous of her own sister.

'Kyla? Don't you think that would be a good plan?'

She swayed a little, blinking as she realised they were all looking at her. What had they been talking about? 'Oh, I'm sorry.' She managed a rueful smile. 'My mind wandered there for a sec. What did you say, Nairne?'

'Adam's friendly with the new owner of Pozzi's. He

suggested taking Kevin to look for a bike while you and I go into Albert's Tearoom for a coffee.'

Adam was looking down at her, waiting for her answer. 'Oh,' she frowned, 'I don't think Kevin would go without me, but thanks for suggesting it. I appreci-ate——'

'Mom. . .'

Kyla raised her eyebrows as she felt Kevin tugging at her coat. 'What is it, sweetie?'

His eyes were sparkling eagerly. 'Wanna go. With. . .' He blushed shyly. 'With Adam.'

'You. . .you do?' Kyla could hardly believe her ears. 'Well, wonderful! But do you have time, Adam?'

Adam grinned easily and made a dismissing gesture. 'I always do my banking on a Monday morning, and Nairne and I have got into the habit of going to Albert's for coffee before I go back to Redhillock. You two haven't had much of a chance to talk. This'll be a good opportunity for you.'

He took his arm from around Nairne's shoulder and said to Kevin, 'How about giving me your hand?'

'A bike with training wheels, Adam,' Kyla called after them helplessly. 'How about if you let Kevin choose one and have them put it aside and I'll look at it later, before we go home?'

'You've got it!' Adam threw them a cheery smile and shortened his stride so that Kevin could keep up with him as they walked along the street.

'Now,' Nairne suggested, 'let's go for that cup of coffee before we freeze to death.'

Albert's Tearoom was half a block away in the opposite direction from Pozzi's, and as Kyla strolled along the pavement with Nairne she mustered all the self-control she could find. Nairne had always been extremely sensi-tive to other people's feelings. Everything Kyla had achieved five years ago with her betrayal—tender though it had been—would be in jeopardy, might actually have been in vain, if Nairne were to guess that Kyla had never stopped loving Adam.

She looked up at the low, ragged clouds slouching their way across the sombre sky. Was there *never* going to be an end to the deception?

They were fortunate to find an empty table. Albert's was crowded, but an elderly couple had just vacated a window-table as Nairne and Kyla walked through the bakery at the front and entered the tearoom.

'Albert's is the "in" place in Glencraig at the moment, Kyla.' Nairne slid her green coat over the back of her seat. 'They have the best coffee in town, and their cakes and scones are second to none.'

Kyla tried to concentrate on her surroundings, forcing out of her mind the vivid picture of Adam and Kevin strolling along the street together. She slipped off her burgundy jacket and drew in a deep, calming breath. 'It's super—nice and bright.'

The mirrored walls, gleaming black and white tiled floor, and crisp linen tablecloths contrasted charmingly with the sprigs of red-berried holly adorning the centre of each table. Wonderful fragrances wafted through the tearoom. There was the aroma of the coffee, of course, and the delicious smell of the freshly baked morning rolls and bread coming from the bakery, but Kyla could also detect the light floral perfumes of the matrons sitting nearby in their wool sweaters, tweed skirts and pearls, could almost smell the powder and lipstick from each perfectly made-up face. Everywhere she glanced, she could see people smiling to her, or giving a little wave of their coffee-cup.

'You probably know everyone here,' Nairne murmured before turning to the waitress who had come to take their order. 'What will you have, Kyla? Tea or coffee?'

'Coffee, please, and. . .mm. . .a custard slice, I think.'

'I'll bring a plate of cakes, ma'am.' The waitress turned to Nairne. 'You'll be having coffee too, Miss Drummond?'

'Thanks, Maisie.'

Kyla chewed nervously on her lip as she looked out to the street. Nairne appeared quite at ease, while she herself was trying desperately to think of something to say. Distractedly she let her gaze drift with the passers-by outside. Young mothers pushing high prams strolled past, their plump, rosy-faced babies propped up against fancy frilled pillows. Older women rushed along in heavy coats and jackets, a strained look on their faces as they did their shopping. Once in a while a man stepped by, smart in a grey suit, or a Burberry raincoat, on his way to car or office. Nothing much had changed in the past five years, though Kyla could see that some of the shops had closed down; their windows were boarded up, and in the doorways teenagers hung around, faces sullen, shoulders hunched.

'There's a lot of unemployment here, as there is all over Scotland.' Nairne's serious voice interrupted Kyla's musings, and she felt herself relax a little as she realised that Nairne had chosen a neutral topic. Was it possible that Nairne wasn't aware of the tension that Kyla felt in the air?

'These lads over there——' Nairne pointed to a large boarded-up doorway across the street '—all used to work at McPhail's Construction. They were laid off months ago, and there's nothing else for them. So they hang around during the day. . .and then get into trouble at night.'

Kyla murmured an absent-mined 'Thank you,' as the waitress laid their coffee-pots and plate of cakes on the table. 'Trouble? What sort of trouble?'

Nairne's mouth pinched thoughtfully as she pushed

the cream jug and sugar bowl over to Kyla. 'Breaking into houses and cars, mainly.' She shrugged. 'They need money, of course, but I don't think that's the whole reason.'

'What is, then?' Kyla knew nothing about the modern teenager. In Toronto, she had lived in the same house for five years, but had barely got to know her neighbours. Some of them had children of high-school age, but Kyla knew nothing of their problems, if they had any.

'Most of these kids come from broken homes, but that's almost the norm now. No, I think the real reason is boredom.' Nairne stirred some sugar into her coffee and handed the plate of cakes to Kyla. 'Here, have a custard slice. There are four on the plate.' She flashed her sister a quick mischievous smile. 'We can have two each.'

'Boredom?'

Nairne toyed distractedly with her knife as she said, 'Rory and I see it all the time, Kyla. Boys getting into trouble simply because they have nothing else to do. They don't have any goals.' She shivered. 'Be sure you don't walk downtown here on your own at night. It's quite frightening. These kids have knives, and they don't hesitate to use them if they get a notion. And of course some of them do drugs and——'

'Heavens, Nairne, and are these the people you're working with every day?' The delicious custardy confection melting in Kyla's mouth lost its flavour. 'Aren't you sacred to *death*?'

Nairne took a slow sip of her coffee. 'No, not really. Rory and I are desperately trying to do something for them. Trying to find something for them to do.' She expelled a heavy breath. 'There's no money. If only we had some money. . .'

The waitress paused to ask if everything was all right, and after she'd passed Kyla asked, 'What would you do if you had money? I mean, there's no point in *giving* them money, is there?'

'Oh, hell, no! Oops—sorry.' Nairne grimaced. 'But you're right. No point at all. They've got to be made to feel good about themselves. Rory and I have this dream. . .'

Nairne placed her hands on the edge of the table in front of her and pushed her chair back. 'Sorry again, Kyla. Here I go on my soapbox!' She wiped her mouth with a corner of her serviette. 'Let's talk about something more cheerful.'

'No, I want to hear.' Kyla couldn't help noticing how Nairne's thin, freckled face had glowed when she talked about the dream she and Rory shared. Something that important to her sister was something she wanted to know more about. 'Tell me.'

Nairne shrugged. 'Remember Bruach?'

'Bruach?' Kyla frowned, absently pouring a second cup of coffee from her pot. 'Oh, Bruach.' Her face cleared. 'That wonderful old house on top of the brae at the opposite end of town from Tigh Na Mara? Away in behind the trees, rather like a castle, with its tower and the maze in the gardens?'

'Yes,' Nairne said eagerly, 'that's the one. It's been empty for five years, and the owners want to sell.' She twisted her lips wryly. 'Of course, no one wants to buy it. It needs so much work. But——' she leaned her elbows on the table, and stared dreamily at Kyla '—if Rory and I could buy it, we could turn it into a project for the local lads. Oh, we haven't worked it out in detail, because it's just a dream, but we could organise the boys into teams, and hire a foreman to show them what to do. They could fix it up—the house first, and then the gardens; the land is first-rate—they could grow vegetables and flowers and send them south. Bruach itself could be run as a bed and breakfast place in summer, and——'

'It sounds *wonderful*, Nairne. And you're right about the boys. It would give them a sense of pride, once they knew they could accomplish something like that. I——'

'Well, still gabbing! Tut, tut, Kevin. What do you think of that? We've been out doing men's work, choosing a bike, and all these women can——'

'Mom, Mom, it's red, and has two big wheels, and two little wheels, and a black seat. . .and a bell!'

Kyla looked round, startled, to find Kevin at her elbow, his little face flushed, his eyes bright with excitement, and behind him Adam, who was looking at Nairne with a warm expression in his eyes. She felt her thoughts darting around in a flurry, trying to cope with everything. She had wanted to hear more about Nairne's dream, but she was so astonished at the transformation in Kevin's attitude, she couldn't concentrate on anything else.

'Mom, come and see it. The man's going to keep it if we go back and pay for it. . .'

Kyla flashed a glance at Adam, to find that he was nodding ruefully. 'I'm afraid you'll have to hurry. Fred says every child in Glencraig wants a bike like that for Christmas. It's the last one he has in the store; he promised to hold it for you if you go straight over.'

'You'll stay and have a coffee, Adam?' Nairne smiled up at Adam as he helped Kyla on with her jacket.

He paused with his hands at her shoulders, his fingertips touching the nape of her neck as he answered, 'Sure, catch Maisie's eye and tell her to bring another pot.'

Kyla felt a tingle ripple down her spine as she felt the firm, casual touch on her skin, and she trembled as she was trapped within the sphere of his magnetism. Out of the corner of her eye she saw Nairne lean back in her chair and wave to Maisie, but her senses were inflamed by Adam's closeness as he brushed a smoothing hand between her shoulder-blades after she slid her arms into her jacket. She could feel his palm in the small of her back, and though she was sure he wasn't even aware of it, it was creating havoc with her senses.

She tightened her jaw as she looked up into his face. 'Thanks for taking Kevin to the bike shop, Adam. You've really made a hit with him.' His eyes were blue and hazy, like smoky clouds in a summer sky. In the brief moment before she bent to take Kevin's hand she saw each separate long black eyelash, all the tiny grey flecks in the iris, and the dark navy ring that circled it. And in that flash she saw a reflection of herself, pale and drawn.

Adam's voice seemed to come from far away. 'Now that you've seen Alex Gordon, we'll have to get together. If I ask nicely this time,' a twinkle cleared the smoke from his eyes suddenly, 'will you drop by the office this afternoon?'

Kyla cleared her throat. How disarming he was when he smiled. 'All right. Kevin goes down for a sleep around one-thirty. How about if I drop by about two?'

'Fine. See you then.'

'Come on, Mom, we're gonna be too late!'

As she and Kevin walked along the pavement a few minutes later, she glanced into the window of the tearoom to wave goodbye, but she needn't have bothered. Nairne and Adam seemed engrossed in each other, and oblivious to the rest of the world.

By the time they reached the bike shop, Kevin was asking innocently, 'Why are you rubbing your eyes, Mom? Did something go in them?'

CHAPTER EIGHT

It was almost two miles by road from Glencraig House to the distillery. Kyla had intended driving there, but when she closed the back door behind her that afternoon she decided it would do her good to walk. Looping the strap of her bag over her shoulders, she strolled towards the barred gate that led to a short cut through the fields.

The prospect of being alone with Adam had made her nerves ragged, but as she swung the gate back into place the beauty of the scenery ensnared her senses. The snow sparkled and twinkled in the sunshine like tinsel, the shaggy coats of Highland cattle daubed the white-blanketed fields with rust, and she found her spirits rising despite her anxiety. She paused for a moment, hardly able to believe that the responsibility for this huge estate rested on her now. The low bleating of unseen sheep and the sad cry of a distant whaup echoed in her ears as she looked down to the hollow below. There, adjacent to the smooth, pewter grey of the dam, sprawled the distillery, its tall, tapering chimney stack and distinctive pagoda-kiln dominating the slate-roofed complex.

As she continued on her way, her boots made a satisfying crunching sound on the barley bristles hidden under the snow, and the fragrance of wood smoke drifting in the air soothed her with its pungent, evocative fragrance. By the time she reached the distillery, she realised that the rough edges of her apprehension had been smoothed.

As the door of the main building clicked shut behind her, Adam appeared at the far end of the corridor. Kyla's steps faltered briefly, the breath catching in her throat at the unexpected sight of his tall, straight-shouldered figure. She had no control over the tingles of excitement that rippled through her. . .like a wave of applause at the sight of a masterpiece, she mused self-derisively.

He hadn't seen her; his head was bent over an open folder in his hand, his brow furrowed as he strode rapidly into the office across the hall. Expelling her breath, Kyla started walking again, her boots echoing softly in the empty corridor.

Just as she approached the end, Adam appeared again. This time he saw her, and he came to an abrupt stop. He was sliding a pencil behind his ear, and his hand halted, suspended in the air while they looked at each other.

Breaking what seemed like an endless, awkward silence, Kyla finally murmured, 'Am I late? I meant to drive, but it was such a lovely day, I walked down through the fields.'

Her heart sank as their eyes met. How on earth was she ever going to hide her feelings from him? He was so dear to her. . .

Adam slid the pencil through the crisp black hair curling over the top of his ear. 'No, you're in good time. I'm the one who's running late. It's been hectic. If one more person calls——'

'Mr Garvie?' A plump blonde in a red tartan dress poked her head round the door of the office Adam had just left. 'There's a Mr Paton on the line. Says it's——'

Kyla raised her eyebrows as Adam swung away into his own office and came out again, flinging his sheepskin jacket over his shoulders. 'Meggie, I'm going out with Mrs Ferguson.'

The young girl gaped at Kyla, then smiled tentatively. 'Oh, righto, I'll just——'

'Take a message, and tell him I'll call him back.'

Before she knew what was happening, Kyla was outside with Adam, and she was standing blinking in the sun.

'We'll never get a chance to talk in there.' He threw

an impatient glance over his shoulder. 'Besides, as you say, it's far too good a day to be indoors. Let's go for a walk, and maybe the fresh air will clear my head. It feels as if it's filled with cement!'

The grey eyes that looked down at her were inscrutable, but Kyla breathed a sigh of relief. She had been dreading being shut up at close quarters with Adam. Surely if they were out of doors, walking while they talked, she could manage to avoid eye contact and maintain an easy, casual dialogue with him?

'Great!' She shielded her eyes from the watery rays of the sun as she looked along the distillery road. 'Shall we go that way, by the water?'

Moments later, they were strolling along a narrow double-tracked path. On one side, skirted by reeds, was the dam—fed year-round by the cold, clear waters of the Craigie Burn—on the other thick masses of whins and gorse, with straggly bramble and wild rose-bushes tangled together under clumps of snow.

'You talked with Alex Gordon this morning?' Adam absently took the pencil from above his ear and tucked it into the pocket of his jacket. 'He explained your options?'

Kyla kicked a lump of snow off the track as she answered. 'Yes, basically he gave me two: sell. . .or keep Whisky Ferguson going, with you as manager.' Concern for Adam pushed aside her tingling awareness of his closeness, and she frowned as she asked, 'Adam, if I do sell, where does that leave you? The contract you made with Barclay, what does it stipulate in the event that——?'

'In the event that Whisky Ferguson falls into other hands?' Adam shrugged. 'In that event, my services will no longer be required. Of course, a new owner might decide to retain me, but I can't count on that.'

Kyla walked for a few moments without responding. She had felt locked in, pressured, knowing that she and

Adam would have to work together. It had never occurred to her that there would be a way out, rather than waiting till the end of his five-year contract. But if she sold the still, and Adam lost his position, would it affect the standard of living he and Nairne were looking forward to?

'What would you advise me to do, Adam? Or is it difficult for you to do that objectively?'

They had reached an open gate and Adam halted, leaning back with his elbows hooked over the top bar. 'The whisky industry on the whole suffered because of the rising popularity of other drinks. You probably saw signs of that as you drove north—thousand upon thousand of empty casks piled high out in the fields.' He raised his eyebrows in Kyla's direction and she nodded.

'Alex and I talked about that,' she said, 'and he told me Barclay was one of the first to foresee the way things were going. He also said that Ferguson Whisky actually had a fifty per cent increase in sales last year.'

Adam squinted against the rays of the sun. 'Barclay was a very astute businessman. At just the right time he invested a lot of money in a major marketing campaign. . .'

As they sauntered along the path and began tramping up the gently sloped field, Kyla was aware that Adam was still speaking, but his words—'new packaging. . .heavily advertised. . .inroads abroad'—barely registered on her mind. In a few minutes they would be reaching the secret sheltered spot under a stand of birch trees where she and Adam used to meet. . .the place where she had ended their engagement, the place where he had stood when he'd flung her antique ruby ring into the heather.

'Mr Gaa. . .aarvie. . .'

The faint call carried across the still air very clearly, interrupting Adam and causing them both to glance round.

'Dammit, did I not tell the woman to take a message?' Adam's expression darkened as he glanced at Kyla for confirmation. 'What the devil do you think she wants?'

Kyla bit back a smile. The blonde secretary, Meggie, her tartan dress like a red flag against the snow, was waving madly in their direction from the far side of the dam. 'I haven't the foggiest, but I guess you'd better find out.'

'Wait here. I'll be right back.'

'I'll walk on slowly,' Kyla replied. 'You can catch me up.'

Dismissing the secretary from her mind, Kyla turned again towards the clump of birch trees about a mile further on. It was a very private place, situated in such a manner that she and Adam could spot intruders long before they themselves could be seen.

She was glad in a way that Adam had been called back. It was her first visit here since the day she'd told him she was breaking their engagement and was going to marry Drew.

It had been a perfect afternoon in June; the singing of the birds, hauntingly beautiful, had torn at her heart. She had known that it would be the last time she'd meet Adam here, and when she had trudged up over the last ridge and had seen him rising from where he lay sprawled lazily under one of the trees she had felt physically sick.

She had walked towards him with her hands behind her back, the fingers of the right tugging blindly at the ring on her left. . .

He knew immediately that something was wrong.

'What is it, Kyla? Aren't you well?' He reached out to her, but she shook her head.

'No, I'm all right.' She had been wearing a pink cotton sun-dress with thin straps that tied in a bow at her shoulders, and the sun was so hot on her back that she was sure she'd be burned. She stood staring at him, knowing that she'd never forget how he looked. His blue shirt was open at the neck, the crisp black hair dark at the V-opening. He stood on the slope above her, and so he appeared taller and broader than ever. His legs, muscular and strong, were astride, his hands in his pockets. As she looked up into his anxious grey eyes, so disarmingly honest, she felt as if her heart were breaking.

'Here, come and sit down. . .'

When she shook her head again, his frown deepened, and she saw his jaw tighten. She knew she had to tell him, quickly, and then leave.

'I. . .I'm going to break our engagement.'

The ring finally slipped off her finger, and she laid it in the palm of her left hand, staring at it as if trying to print the image indelibly on her mind. It was such a beautiful ring. The ruby, nestled in its elaborate silver filigree setting, glowed with crimson extravagance in the sunlight. 'Here, take it.'

He stood looking at her, blankly, so that she wondered if he hadn't heard what she said. She saw him blink, and sway slightly as if he were drunk. Then his head tilted, the way it would if he hadn't understood, and he shook it disbelievingly. A plane droned overhead, its lazy sound contrasting sharply with the intensity of the passion throbbing in the air.

Kyla had meant to give the ring and leave, but all of a sudden she started talking, babbling in an attempt to release the tension between them. 'It's Drew, you see. We. . .I. . .well, you must know that he's always been in love with me, and somehow, I'd never seen him in that light. . .I'd always thought of him as. . .more of a brother. Till he and Nairne got engaged.' Her throat had clogged with emotion and it was painful to swallow. 'It wasn't till I realised I'd almost lost him, that I knew that I. . .' She cleared the huskiness from her voice and fixed her gaze on one of the birch trees behind Adam. 'I knew that it was Drew I loved. We're going to be married, as soon as possible. So will you take the ring back? I'm so sorry, Adam, I hope I haven't hurt you too much. . .'

He didn't lose his temper, didn't start shouting at her, as she had expected.'

It was much worse. He walked over to her, and she jerked her gaze back to his face. The contempt in his eyes made her shrink away from him as he picked the ring from the palm of her outstretched hand.

Without looking where it was going, he flung the ring away into the heather, the only communication between them being the slightest flicker of his lashes when she uttered a loud, involuntary gasp of horror.

Before she had time to protest, he turned away from her and bounded down the hill, shoulders rigid beneath his blue shirt and——

'Kyla!'

Kyla jumped as she felt rough fingers pull at her arm. She swivelled round to look straight into Adam's face, her heart lurching in alarm as she saw the troubled expression in his grey eyes. For a confused moment, she thought she was still in the past, and he had just flung away the ring—till she looked down and saw the snow clumped like melted white marshmallows on the heather.

What had happened? What had Meggie wanted?

'Problems at the still, Adam?' She reached out involuntarily to touch him.

'No, it was you Meggie wanted, not me.' His voice was urgent. 'It's your father. He's had an accident.' His arm curved round her quickly to support her as her knees began to buckle. 'That concoction—whatever it was that he's been working on—backfired. Kate was phoning from the hospital. She needs you there right away.'

'Oh, Adam. . .' Kyla felt her head spin, her senses scatter as panic assailed her. 'What——'

'Come on.' His voice was grim as he led her back towards the distillery. 'I'll drive you.'

* * *

Adam swung the Rover to a stop by the front steps of Glencraig County Hospital, and Kyla jumped out, not taking time to close the passenger door. Seconds later she was running to the reception desk, her boots clattering noisily on the tiled floor.

The next few moments were a blur of white uniforms, antiseptic smells, and brisk, reassuring voices. Then someone led her to a small office, and as the door closed behind her she saw her mother, drained of all her vitality, talking to a young doctor in a green gown.

Kate's large brown eyes glistened with tears as she returned Kyla's hug. 'Oh, darlin', thank heavens that you're here. Your father——'

'What happened, Kate? Can I see him?'

Midnight in Paris mingled with the distinctive hospital smell as her mother flicked back her long braid. 'It exploded, that damn. . .oh!' Words failed her and she began pacing the small room. 'Splinters of metal everywhere. Lucky he is that his face escaped. But he has a nasty gash in his neck. . .And no, we can't see him just now. He's being prepared for surgery. Dr Stuart tells me—oh, sorry, Doctor, this is our older girl, Kyla. . .Kyla, Dr Stuart—the doctor tells me your dad may need a blood transfusion.'

'Hello, Kyla.' The doctor, fresh-faced and sandy-haired, clasped Kyla's hand briefly in his. Alert, bespectacled eyes looked down into hers. 'Yes, your mother's right. Your father may need some blood. Now that you're here, we can find out if your blood type is compatible and——'

'Blood type? Does Dad need a transfusion?'

Kyla twisted round as she heard Nairne's voice behind her. Outside the door she caught a glimpse of Rory and Adam, then it swung shut, and Nairne crossed the room, the emerald green of her coat startling in the pristine white hospital surroundings.

Her eyes were distraught, her hair disarrayed. 'Sorry

I couldn't get here sooner, Mum. Rory and I were out at——'

'Your Dad may need blood, and Dr Stuart was asking Kyla what her blood type is. He was hoping that——'

'Oh, let me!' Nairne tugged off her coat and flung it over a chair, her pale cheeks flushing. 'Where do I go? I want to be the one. If my blood's compatible, I want Dad to have it——'

She was at the door, pulling it open, and waiting impatiently for the doctor to follow her.

Dr Stuart lifted a folder from his desk and crossed the room. 'I'll take you to the lab, Nairne. Are you coming, Mrs Drummond? Then——'

Kyla closed her eyes, wondering if she was going to faint. As she heard the door close behind them, thoughts swirled round and round in her head till it was ready to burst.

She didn't know too much about blood types. She *did* know that a blood test couldn't prove positively that a man *was* the father of a particular child. . .but she also knew that blood tests could prove positively that a man *was not*. . .*could not* be the father of that child. She felt her pulses thud frighteningly fast as she brought her thoughts to an inescapable conclusion. If Nairne gave a blood sample that was not compatible with Malcolm Drummond's, it might also prove conclusively that she couldn't be Malcolm Drummond's daughter. If the doctor blurted out something in his surprise. . .

'Oh, no, she moaned aloud. Her thoughts spun round in circles. She couldn't allow it to happen. Nairne mustn't ever find out. She had to do something. And she would have to move fast; she had wasted enough time already.

Her heartbeats skidded as she opened her eyes. Standing across the room, staring at her in utter dismay, was Kate. She hadn't hurried away with Nairne and the doctor as Kyla had believed. She had been right here all the time. . .had seen her reaction, had heard her tortured murmur of protest.

In the shocked silence that hummed between them, a sing-song anonymous voice called one of the doctors on the PA system: 'Dr Matthews to Room 14, Dr Matthews, please, right away. . .'

Kyla saw the colour drain from her mother's face, saw her brown eyes widen with horror—horror at the knowledge that Kyla knew her secret? Horror that Nairne might be on the verge of learning the truth? Kyla had no time to stay and find out. . .no *wish* to stay and find out. . .

'I've got to stop Nairne. . .' She brushed past Kate's outstretched hand as she ran to the door. 'I've——'

'Wait!' Her mother's voice implored her. 'I want——'

Kyla stumbled out into the corridor, slamming the door shut behind her and almost colliding with Rory and Adam.

'Where did they go?' she asked fiercely. 'Nairne and the doctor, did you see?'

Adam swiftly scanned her face. 'This way.' Kyla felt her hand grabbed in his. 'Here, I'll take you.'

He strode, and she ran with him, along corridors that seemed endless. When they finally reached the lab, Kyla's lungs felt as if they were on fire. Through the glass door, she could see Nairne, Dr Stuart, and an assistant in a white jacket.

'Adam——' she paused breathlessly for a fraction of a second with the doorknob in her hand '—I want you to take Nairne back to Dr Stuart's office. Kate needs her. Wait here for just a minute.'

Without giving him time to reply, she pushed past him into the room. Breath rasping in her throat, she leaned back against the glass panelled door.

'Dr Stuart,' she blurted, 'what blood type is my dad?' The doorhandle jutted painfully into her back as she waited for his answer, intensely aware that all three were staring at her, their expressions perplexed.

The doctor jammed his hands into the pockets of his green uniform. 'Type A.' His glasses glinted under the harsh lighting, his sandy brows twisted in a frown.

Kyla's breath shuddered out noisily. 'So's mine. You won't have to bother testing Nairne. I'll be able to give blood if my father needs it.'

She saw Nairne's eyes widen in an expression of hurt and incredulity. 'But, Kyla, I want to. I'd do anything for Dad, you know that. And this is such an opportunity. Oh, it's a small thing, but it means such a lot to me——'

Kyla moved quickly to her side, gave her a swift hug. 'It means a lot to me too, Nairne. And Dr Stuart did ask me first,' she reminded her with a lightness she didn't feel. 'So why don't you and Adam go sit with Kate? This won't take too long, I shouldn't imagine. Then I'll come and join you.'

Nairne raised her hands in an appealing gesture, then slowly dropped them. 'All right.' Her voice was laced with resentment. 'If it's so important to you. . .'

She sidestepped Kyla, eyes averted, and muttering a low, 'Sorry, Dr Stuart,' ran out of the room.

In the awkward silence she left behind, Kyla turned to the doctor with a wan smile. 'Right,' she murmured wearily, 'let's not waste any more time. Shall we get on with it?'

'. . .and when Cheeky Chicken got to the edge of the lake, he saw a mother duck in the water. She had six ducklings with her, and they were swimming in a straight line. Five of them were yellow, but the smallest one, the one at the end. . .'

Kyla turned the page of the picture book and continued reading to Kevin, but though her arm was round the pyjamaed figure cuddled in her lap in front of the drawing-room fire, and though every now and then she stopped to plant a kiss on top of his fair head, her mind was miles away. . .

The atmosphere in the waiting-room when she'd returned from the lab had been so strianed, she had almost turned and walked out again. Nairne and Rory were sitting together on a sofa, Rory sipping coffee from a styrofoam cup and Nairne flicking through the pages of a magazine, but quite obviously not reading it. Rory threw her a quiet smile when she came in, but Nairne didn't look up. Adam was leaning against the wall, hands thrust tautly into the side pockets of his cords, and he did look at Kyla. His grey eyes had never seemed quite as hard, quite as impenetrable, Kyla thought miserably as she took a seat by the door. She tried not to meet Kate's eyes. Her mother was pacing back and forth, back and forth across the small waiting-room with her fingers twined together in front of her, as if in prayer.

No one had spoken till Dr Stuart had come to tell them that his patient was now in the recovery-room, that the shards of metal had all been removed, and that Mac would be fine.

'You'll be relieved to know that he didn't require a transfusion, after all. But I'm sure,' he went on with a smile, seemingly unaware of the tension his remarks caused, 'he'll be delighted to learn that his two daughters were vying with each other to give him some blood!'

'Can I see him, Dr Stuart?' Kate's fingers were at her cheeks now. 'Is he still under the anaesthetic?'

The doctor glanced round. 'I think the rest of you should go on home. Come back in the morning, if you like. Mrs Drummond, you'll be able to see your husband in about quarter of an hour. . .but just for a few minutes. I'll come and get you,' he added as he swung open the door and left.

Kyla watched miserably as Nairne kissed Kate on the cheek. 'Rory drove me here, Mum, so I'll have to go back to the office with him to get the Morris. Shall I come and pick you up?' Her red hair shimmered under the lights as she turned to Kyla and added abruptly, 'Can we drop you off?'

Adam's deep voice broke in before either Kate or Kyla could answer. 'Why don't you go straight to Tigh Na Mara from the office, Nairne, and get the supper started? Kate's not going to feel like cooking tonight. I'll drive Kate and Kyla both home.'

Kate patted Adam's arm. 'That's kind of you.' She ushered Nairne and Rory to the door. 'We can have a mixed grill—there are some nice sausages in the fridge, and kidney, and chops. . .'

As soon as Rory and Nairne had left, Kate turned to Adam. 'Would you mind getting us some coffee, Adam? I didn't feel like it earlier, but now that Mac is going to be all right. . .You'll find a coffee machine by the front door. Miles away. . .hope it doesn't get stone cold by the time you come back. . .' She curled her lips into a coaxing smile—a smile which faded away completely as soon as she and Kyla were left alone.

'We've got to talk, Kyla. . .This isn't the place I would have chosen, nor the time, but——'

Kyla felt a cold shiver ice her spine as she saw the deathly white of her mother's cheeks. It was only two days ago, for the first time in her life, that she had seen her mother cry. Now she saw the jaunty Irish sprite crumple completely. At last Kate looked every day of her fifty years.

'Oh, Kyla, how long have you known?' The petite figure stumbled back and slumped into one of the chairs, her fingers pressed to her cheeks. 'Tell me.'

Kyla let her gaze slide away from her mother's pathetically searching eyes. 'Kate, it doesn't matter now, everything's all right. Mac didn't need blood——'

'Tell me!'

Kate's voice was thick with pain. Kyla could hardly

bear it; was the only way to ease the burden to tell her what she wanted to know?

She looked at her steadily. 'I knew before I left.'

Kate looked at Kyla as if she'd stabbed her in the heart. 'Holy Mother of God! So it's true.' She shook her head from side to side in a futile gesture of denial. 'These past five years, I've hoped. . .and prayed. . .that it wasn't so.' Hugging her thin arms around herself, she asked in a choked voice, 'How. . .how did you find out?'

Kyla felt her throat constrict with emotion, but she swallowed and forced herself to speak. 'I happened to pick up the phone in my office when you and. . . Barclay were talking, the day Nairne and Drew got engaged——'

She heard Kate draw in a sharp hissing breath. 'So that was what happened. I racked my brains but could never come up with an answer. But why did you have to——'

'Kate——' Kyla's tone was shrill '——I really don't want to talk about it.'

'I've got to know.' Her mother's large brown eyes swam beseechingly. 'Don't you understand?'

A resentful retort sprang to Kyla's lips, but she bit it back. What was to be gained by making Kate feel more guilty than she already did? 'Yes,' she admitted heavily, 'I understand.' Hardly aware of what she was doing, she twisted her wedding band round and round on her finger. 'I acted the way I did because I felt I had no other choice.' Strangely enough, now that she had started talking, she found she wanted to go on, to spill out all the things that up till now she could never share with anyone. 'After I overheard your conversation, I biked up to the head of the loch and stayed there for a long time, trying to sort out my emotions. Images whirled round and round in my head like a reel of film that had snapped and was spinning out of control.' The memory was so clear it made her shudder. 'Eventually,' she went on, 'I knew what I had to do. I told Adam I wasn't going to marry him, and then I——'

'And then you went to Drew.' Kate sounded a hundred years old. 'You told him that when you heard he was engaged to Nairne, you suddenly realised it was him you loved, not Adam. And Drew, of course, having blindly adored you all his life, just as blindly accepted your story.'

Kyla tried to smile, but her lips were stiff. 'Drew believed me because he *wanted* to believe me. He'd proposed to Nairne on the rebound—impulsively, because he felt thwarted. He'd been wanting to marry me for ages—he'd always insisted we were meant for each other and that it was only a matter of time before I realised it. But how did you guess it happened like that?'

Kate brushed the back of her hand across her eyes. 'Oh, darlin', I know you so well. . .and I also knew Drew. He was a likeable lad, but Barclay completely spoiled him after his mother died. He was used to demanding his own way—and getting it!'

Kyla stilled her trembling fingers by twining them together at her waist. 'I wanted to put as much distance between him and Nairne as possible, so I suggested we should go abroad and make a fresh start. He asked his father to transfer him to the Ferguson Whisky office in Toronto. Of course,' she added with an edge of bitterness, 'Barclay jumped at the idea. Oh, I *hated* deceiving Drew! We'd always been such good friends. But the only option was to tell him what I'd found out. . .and apart from the fact that I didn't feel it was my secret to share, I just couldn't take that risk. I was terrified he might insist Nairne had a right to know the truth.' Kyla threaded her fingers through her hair distraughtly. 'Oh, Kate, my actions might not seem logical, but at the time my thoughts were anything but logical. I was in shock. . .and more than half-mad with worry! You know how I doted on Nairne, and you know how innocent and vulnerable she was at seventeen. I honestly didn't think she could cope with knowing that you. . .that she. . .' Kyla's words trailed away into silence. She didn't speak for a moment, and then she said with fierce defiance, 'I'd have married Old Nick himself to protect her!'

Kate flung her hands out in a helpless gesture. 'And you're *still* trying to protect her. Oh, if only——'

'Kate,' Kyla responded tautly, 'all the "if only"s in the world can't change anything now. As Dad would say, it's water under the bridge!'

Kate took the hem of her smock and wiped her cheek. For a long moment, the only sound in the room was a burst of cheery laughter from the hallway beyond the closed door. When Kate finally spoke, it was to say in a low, shaky tone, 'I don't know what I would have done if Nairne had given blood and——'

'I know.' Kyla's voice echoed the dread in her mother's. 'The blood tests might have revealed. . .' Oh, even now, now that her mother knew she shared her secret, she couldn't bring herself to say it. . .

'. . .reveal that Mac isn't Nairne's father.' Kate's words were a bare whisper. 'Oh, Kyla, let me tell you how it happened. You have a right to know.' She pushed herself to her feet, holding on to the back of the chair for support. 'When——'

'No!' Kyla thrust out with her hands as if she could physically shut out the sound of her mother's voice. 'No, I don't want to know!'

But her mother went on as if she hadn't heard her. 'It all happened so very long ago. Barclay and his wife, Hilda, were my two dearest friends. I'll never forget the day of Hilda's funeral. . .Barclay was out of his mind with grief. Your father was away on a fishing trip, and Barclay came to Tigh Na Mara in the middle of the night. He was talking about killing himself, swearing that he couldn't go on. Oh, I tried my best to talk him out of it, took him in my arms, rocked him like a baby. . .'

Kyla leaned back against the door, feeling as if she were dreaming. It was quite obvious to her that her mother had completely forgotten she was in the room. She was talking to herself, just as she might have done all those years ago, when, alone with her little baby girl, Kyla herself, her husband away at sea, she did her best to comfort a dear friend who was threatening to take his life. . .

'. . .and it was an act of mercy. It truly was. Somehow it was the only thing that convinced Barclay that he had a friend who would do anything, anything at all, to keep him alive.' Kate sighed suddenly, and blinking, looked round. She smiled to Kyla. 'And then nine months later, Nairne was born. Barclay knew she was his. I didn't ever have to tell him. But of course Mac never suspected——'

'Kate, Nairne must never know.' Kyla pushed herself away from the door and took Kate's hands roughly in hers. 'You must promise. She must be protected. . .Promise, Kate!' She gripped the small, slender fingers in hers.

'Don't worry, Kyla.' Kate returned the pressure. 'I promise, she——'

She quickly compressed her lips, and she and Kate sprang apart guiltily as the door burst open.

'Two coffees coming up.' Adam's cheerful voice filled the room. 'I met Dr Stuart. He says you can see Mac now, Kate. Drink your coffee first, and while you're with him, I'll run Kyla to Glencraig House, then I'll come back for you.'

It was with some reluctance that Kyla accepted Adam's brusque offer to drive her home. Though her mind was swirling with the tale Kate had told her, she couldn't help wondering what Adam had made of the little scene he had witnessed through the glass door of the lab. Had Nairne explained it? Had she told him that once again her elder sister had stepped in and taken what she wanted, regardless of other people's feelings?

Whatever she had said, Adam didn't confront Kyla. He drove in silence to the large house, and when Kyla thanked him for his help that afternoon he just nodded curtly, and the moment she closed the car door he put his foot to the accelerator and the black Rover tore away down the hill into the darkness of the afternoon.

Misery had overwhelmed Kyla as she walked along the path to the door. She couldn't stay here, with Nairne despising her, Adam sending her on a roller-coaster of emotions every time they met, Kate making her a confidante concerning the sins of yesterday. . .

No, she couldn't take it any more. She must leave, as soon as possible, and she and Kevin would make a good life somewhere else. Surely in less than a week he hadn't put down enough roots that it would harm him if they went away?

She started as she felt his small hand tug gently at her hair. She had finished the story without realising it. Kevin's mouth opened in a wide yawn, and Kyla smiled down at him tenderly. 'Bed for you, young man! You're late tonight, but that's only because you had such a long sleep this afternoon. Fortunately for Martha,' she added, frowning briefly as she remembered how tired the housekeeper had looked earlier. So much so that Kyla had ordered her to go to her room and rest till the morning.

'Come and I'll give you a piggy-back upstairs.' Kyla sat forward on the couch while Kevin scrambled up onto her shoulders. 'Hold on tight, now.'

When she dropped him on to his bed and tucked him in, Kevin looked up at her, his eyes sleepy. 'Mom, are we going to stay here forever?'

Kyla felt her heart jolt. 'Would you like that, sweetheart?'

He nodded emphatically, another yawn splitting his

face. 'Yes. I like it here. I like Adam. I want to stay forever.'

His eyelids dropped, and he was asleep.

Kyla sank down on to the edge of the bed, her knees suddenly weak. She was well and truly trapped. She had come back to Glencraig for Kevin's sake, in the hope that he would come out of the shell he'd built round himself. And it had worked. Far sooner than she'd expected.

It was what she'd prayed for, but now that it had happened she felt overwhelmed by the ramifications. Oh, she had no doubt that it was the best place for Kevin to be, and he would positively flower under everyone's adoration. But if she stayed she would have to cope with seeing Adam alone on a regular basis while he ran Ferguson Whisky for her. Was there no way she could avoid these business meetings?

But, even as she asked herself the question, the obvious answer thrust itself into her mind: sell the distillery.

If she did, their only contact would be social, and she could make sure that there were always other people around. It would be easy to arrange for Kevin and Adam to have time together during family get-togethers at Tigh Na Mara, and at Redhillock once Adam and Nairne were married.

If she sold the business, it would also solve a problem that had been nagging at her ever since the funeral. Nairne was Barclay's daughter, and she was entitled to a share of his wealth. When she had talked to Kyla about Bruach, the house that Rory and she wanted as a project for the unemployed youths in their area, the germ of an idea had sprouted in Kyla's head. This was Nairne's dream, and Kyla could, with the co-operation of Alex Gordon, help her achieve it.

She got up, aware that much of her depression had lifted. Now that the decision was made to stay in

Glencraig, and she had a sense of purpose, she felt suddenly more energetic. Tomorrow she would put her plan in motion.

The front door bell rang as she crossed the hall, and she walked over to the door, glancing briefly at her reflection in the hallstand mirror. Though she had slipped into a turquoise velvet robe after dinner, it was loose-fitting and quite respectable. Her afternoon walk through the fields had flushed her cheeks, and her eyes sparkled with the satisfaction of knowing that she'd finally made her decision about the future. Fluffing out her long black hair with the back of her hand, she pulled open the door.

Adam, his face haggard and bleak, pushed past her into the hallway before she could protest.

With a rough movement of his arm, he shoved the door shut. His loud breathing was ragged in the quietness of the hallway, and Kyla felt her heartbeats accelerate wildly as she waited for him to speak. When he did, she bit her teeth sharply into her lip till she tasted the warm blood on her tongue.

'What the *hell* is going on?'

He didn't wait for an answer. Kyla flinched as he grabbed her upper arms with his strong fingers and held her away from him so that he could stare straight into her face.

'This afternoon at the hospital Nairne wanted to give blood. Now, as far as I could see, that was no big deal. But *you* made an issue of it. It doesn't make sense, that you would fight with your sister about something like that, considering your claim that you came back to Glencraig to be part of your family again. What did it matter whose blood Mac got, as long as he was going to be all right? But you made it an issue. *And you were out of your mind with worry.* In heaven's name, Kyla, *why? Why* were you so afraid that Nairne would give blood this afternoon? No, dammit, don't try to deny it!' he exploded as Kyla shook her head frantically, her hair swinging over her cheeks. 'You were afraid. I've been going crazy trying to figure out why. And I'm not leaving here till I find out.'

CHAPTER NINE

KYLA'S thoughts swirled in a maelstrom of indecision. She knew Adam meant what he said. He would stay at Glencraig House all night—longer, if necessary—to get at the truth. What was she going to do?

'We can't talk out here. We may waken Kevin.' She twisted herself abruptly from his grip and wheeled away. 'Let's go into the drawing-room.'

She could sense his presence right behind her as she crossed the hall, could hear the firm, relentless tread of his brogues on the carpeted floor as she walked through the open doorway and hesitated by the coffee-table. When she took a deep breath and turned, her nerves vibrated in alarm. Adam was flinging his sheepskin coat over one of the armchairs and she could see that the pressure of his anger had brought into prominence a large vein at his temple. He took up a stance with his back to the fireplace, his arms folded aggressively across his chest, frustration blazing from his grey eyes with the burning intensity of hot coals.

'Would you like something to drink?' Kyla tried to crush back the wave of desperation that was flooding over her. 'Martha's gone to bed, but perhaps I could make you a cup of——'

'I didn't come here to make small talk over a cup of tea.' Adam's harsh tone had the rasping sound of a saw-blade cutting through dry wood. 'And for pity's sake, sit down.' He gestured impatiently with one hand. 'You look like a heron about to take flight.'

Compressing her lips to cut off a quick retort, Kyla lowered herself on to the edge of the couch, and in an effort to avoid Adam's razor-sharp examination let her gaze slide to the companion set on the hearth. Despite her consternation, she willed her mind to come up with a plausible explanation of her actions at the hospital, an explanation that would satisfy Adam.

'I feel very badly about. . .about my behaviour this afternoon.' Her eyelids flickered as she heard a clump of snow crash from the roof on to a bush outside the window. 'I. . .I guess being the elder sister has made me rather bossy, maybe even selfish. And Nairne had had Dad all to herself for the last five years. I wanted to be the one to do something. . .anything. . .to help make up for having stayed away for so long.'

The brass companion set gleamed brightly in the light from the fire, the flat surface of the shovel reflecting the flames in a way that was hypnotic. Kyla couldn't drag her gaze away as she waited tensely for Adam's response.

'Good try, Kyla.' His soft words had the cutting edge of a diamond. 'Good, but not good enough.' He took a step forward, blocking her view of the fire irons. 'And look at me, dammit, when I'm talking to you.' With the toe of his large brogue he kicked out furiously at the cushioned frame of the sofa.

Kyla felt tears burn her eyes. The last few days had been painful as she'd tried to come to grips with her new situation, and now that she had decided to stay in Glencraig she badly needed some time to herself, time to rein in her volatile emotions. But here was Adam, pressuring her for answers—answers that weren't hers to give. Surreptitiously she dabbed at the corner of one eye with a fingertip.

'Are you crying?'

Adam's abrupt question startled her, and she stiffened as he lowered his frame on to the sofa beside her. Firm fingers cupped her jaw, tilting it up.

Like a wild horse unaccustomed to being touched, Kyla jerked her head away, but not before she had seen the remorse in his eyes.

'Good lord, Kyla, you know I can't cope with feminine tears! Just tell me what you're hiding, and I'll leave you alone.'

Kyla's fingers trembled as she searched in the pocket of her robe for a Kleenex and wiped the dampness from her cheeks. She felt cornered, like a mouse shrinking in terror from an angry, unpredictable cat. She had to get rid of him before he succeeded in prying information from her that she didn't want to give!

The fire crackled and spat as she stumbled heavily to her feet.

'Adam, you'll just have to accept my explanation.' Her legs almost gave way under her as she stepped around the coffee-table and moved behind one of the fireside wing-chairs. She clutched the velvety padded crest to support herself. 'You *must* stop trying to read something into what happened at the hospital.'

He pushed himself up from the sofa, his eyes clouded as if what she said hadn't registered with him. With a distracted gesture, he lifted a heavy marble lighter from the coffee-table and rubbed its rounded contours with the pad of his thumb. 'I hate to be in the middle of a situation, and not know what the hell's going on,' he muttered. 'I know something's——'

'Adam, you're wrong!'

He flicked the lighter on, staring unblinkingly at the flaring yellow flame, as if it were the eye of a snake, before extinguishing it again. Kyla sensed his mind was totally preoccupied, trying to solve the puzzle. . .but as long as she guarded her silence he wouldn't have enough pieces to put it together.

And she *would* guard her silence. Confidence surged through her. She would stall, even lie, to allay his suspicions. Even as she congratulated herself on her determination, however, Adam thumped the lighter on to the table-top and his jaw tightened.

'OK, Kyla.' He shrugged his broad shoulders. 'If you

want to play dumb I'm going to have to ask questions elsewhere.' His lips drew back in a thin smile. 'Maybe Nairne can come up with some of the answers that *you're* so loath to give.' He ignored Kyla's swiftly indrawn hiss. 'I think I'll go to Tigh Na Mara now, and have a talk with her.'

Fear constricted Kyla's throat. 'No, Adam,' she said hoarsely, 'you mustn't talk to Nairne. You want answers: all right. . .I admit it. I. . .did have a . . .a reason for acting the way I did this afternoon.'

Strong hands gripped her shoulders, grey eyes swept her up in a fierce gaze.

'So I was right.' His voice was hard and satisfied. 'It wasn't my imagination playing nasty tricks. You say you don't want me to go to Nairne. But what else can I do, if you won't co-operate, my dear Kyla?' His fingers bit into the flesh of her upper arms. 'One way or another I'm going to find out. Tonight.'

Waves of panic washed over Kyla as she gazed beseechingly up at him. 'It won't do any good. You have to understand. . .the answers I spoke about. . .Nairne doesn't have them.' It was hard to meet his brilliant, disbelieving look. 'You'll have to trust me, Adam. If you persist with this, you're going to cause more damage than you can possibly imagine.' Her eyes filled with tears. 'Damage that you'll never be able to repair.'

His hands slid up to her neck, his fingertips reaching to the sensitive skin at her nape, his thumbs pressing against the clean line of her jaw, pulling, so that her lips parted. 'If you give me an explanation that satisfies me, I promise I won't go to Nairne.' He pulled her face so close she could see the beads of perspiration coating his forehead. 'Can you do that?'

Kyla frantically explored her mind, but all she could think of was what might happen if he confronted Nairne. If he revealed that Kyla had a secret reason for preventing her younger sister from giving blood to Mac, Nairne might leave no stone unturned till she found out what that reason was.

'Can you?' Adam's thumbs squeezed against Kyla's temples, as if to force out the answer from her.

'Oh, Adam, I. . .I can't.' Tears rolled down Kyla's cheeks, their warm salitiness curling to the edge of her mouth. 'I——'

With a savage imprecation, he swung away and strode to the door. 'OK. I warned you. . .'

As he wrenched at the handle, Kyla uttered a strangled, 'Wait!'

The command hung between them in the tension-filled room. Adam stared at her, his broad shoulders half turned away, his grey eyes hostile. Very deliberately he clicked the door shut and began walking towards her, his steps smooth and menacing.

Kyla clasped her hands together against her ribcage in an effort to stop the wild sprinting of her heartbeats. As he came closer, she stepped back. 'No.' She held her palms out facing him, like a barrier. 'Don't touch me.'

'Don't worry.' He stood glaring at her. 'I don't intend to. But if this is a trick. . .'

'No.' She slid her hands into the pockets of her robe and took a deep breath. 'No, Adam. I'm going to tell you the truth, but you have to swear never to reveal it to a living soul.'

'You have my word.' He rubbed one hand against the nape of his neck in a fatigued gesture. 'Now, can we get on with it?'

Kyla dipped her eyelids. She just couldn't watch his face change as she revealed Kate's fiercely guarded secret. 'I'm telling you only because you leave me no alternative. I wouldn't be talking to you like this if you hadn't threatened to go to Nairne——'

'For pity's sake, Kyla——'

'All right, all right.' Kyla ran her tongue over her parched lips. How had she let herself be drawn into this position? But there was no way out. She had to protect Nairne, as she always had. . .

'You. . .you guessed there was a reason why I didn't want Nairne to give blood this afternoon. You were right. I was terrified that when the doctor compared her blood type with Dad's, he. . .' She paused for a moment before going on bleakly, 'I don't know if you're aware that there are tests which show conclusively that a man can't possibly be the father of a particular child. I. . .' she stumbled before going on, as she remembered Nairne's eagerness at the hospital, followed by her resentment when Kyla had intervened '. . .I was afraid the doctor might notice something. . .say something that would alert Nairne. . .'

Kyla swallowed. She didn't trust herself to speak for a moment. She could sense Adam's impatience, could almost feel his will urging her on.

'. . .alert her to the fact that she's. . .she's not——' the last words came out in a defiant sob '—she's not Mac's daughter.'

As she spoke, Kyla tilted her chin up and glared at Adam, as if daring him to ask one more question, or make one facetious comment. But for a long moment he didn't say anything, just stared at her, his grey eyes wide and incredulous.

Finally, a deep, low whistle issued from between his lips. 'Hell, I had no idea.' Roughly he rubbed one hand over the back of his head. 'No wonder you were in a panic! How painful and shocking it would have been for Nairne to have found out that way. . .' A faint wave of colour tinged his cheeks. He took a step towards her, and then stopped, fists clenched. 'I've never had any patience with people who jump to conclusions before they know all the facts, but that's exactly what I did this afternoon. I'm sorry, Kyla, I feel so badly for misjudging you——'

'That's all right,' Kyla interjected swiftly. Despite the

fact that Adam had dropped his domineering manner, she could feel tension knotting the muscles of her neck. She knew that he wouldn't be human if he wasn't curious to know who Nairne's real father was. Kyla prayed that not even a suspicion of the truth would whisper its way into his mind. She almost shuddered as she visualised the emotional tangle that would ensue for Nairne, Adam and herself if the truth were revealed. 'You saw something that puzzled you, and you wanted to get to the bottom of it. Now that you have. . .' she made a helpless gesture with her hands '. . .will you just go? I'm really tired——'

Adam frowned, and said slowly, 'I find it hard to believe. When you see Nairne and Mac together, they're so close. Their rapport is. . .unusually strong.' He looked speculatively at Kyla. 'One thing I don't understand is, why do you know, and yet Nairne doesn't? Surely if anyone should have been told, *she* should.'

'No one told me. I found out. . .by accident.'

'I'm not trying to pry into things that are none of my business,' he said carefully, 'but——'

'You're right, Adam,' Kyla snapped. 'It *is* none of your business. You came here demanding to know why I acted as I did at the hospital, and. . .with great reluctance. . .I told you. I've told you all that I'm *going* to tell you, and I'd like to remind you of your promise that the secret won't go any further.'

Adam flashed her a derisive glance. 'You can set your mind at rest on that point. When I make a promise, I keep it.'

Was he thinking about her own broken promises? She felt herself flinch back as he scooped up his coat and strode past her to the door.

He wrenched at the knob. 'But I think you. . .and Kate. . .are making a big mistake. I should think you'd realise, after that episode this afternoon, that someone should tell Nairne before she, like yourself, finds out by accident. . .It's bloody ridiculous that you know yet she doesn't. Nairne's a grown woman. *Mature enough to know the truth.*'

The front door slammed behind him, and Kyla sank on to the couch with an exhausted groan. *The truth.* Oh, if only Adam knew the truth—the whole truth, not just the small part she'd stalled him with.

She leaned back against the cushions and closed her eyes. But he would never know. Only she and Kate knew, and hadn't Kate promised only hours before that the secret would stay safe forever?

Kyla parked the Bentley just inside the hospital grounds the following afternoon. As she and Kevin walked across the lawn towards the red brick building, she glanced up at the seagulls that were swooping with mocking screams under the leaden sky.

'Mom.' Kevin tugged at her hand. 'Isn't that Adam?'

Jerking her head round, Kyla followed Kevin's pointing finger. The heavy entrance doors were swinging shut, and she could see Adam and Nairne walking down the short flight of steps. Heads bent, intent on their conversation, they hadn't noticed Kyla or Kevin.

'You're right, Kev.' Automatically, Kyla adjusted the checked wool scarf at the throat, and smoothed gloved fingers down the front of her taupe raincoat. She tried to ignore the anxious flutter in her chest. 'He's——'

'*Adam!*'

Kevin's spontaneous whoop interrupted Kyla's words, and for a moment she stopped in her tracks as Kevin darted away. A rueful smile curved her lips as she watched his small figure hurtle towards Adam with the single-minded intensity of a jet-propelled rocket, his too-large yellow slicker flapping round his slight body.

She saw Nairne and Adam raise their heads simultaneously, and as she began walking again she heard Adam laugh, heard his chuckled, 'Whoa, young fellow!'

and heard Kevin's shriek of delight as Adam whirled him in the air. Nairne stood back, a cheery grin lighting her delicate features.

'Hi, there.' Kyla reached them just as Adam was dropping Kevin to the ground. 'Have you been to see Dad? How is he?' She waited anxiously for Nairne's response. Was she still resentful? Had Adam said anything to Nairne about having paid a visit to Glencraig House the previous evening? She'd have to tread carefully in case she put her foot in it.

'He's just fine, Kyla, but. . .but before you go to see him——'

Kyla heard Nairne's voice falter, and felt herself stiffen in anticipation.

'Before you go in to see Dad, there's something I want to say.'

Was Nairne going to berate her for her behaviour at the hospital the day before? Nervously Kyla dug the point of one black boot into the ground, but managed to meet Nairne's eyes in a level gaze. 'What about?'

Nairne glanced at Adam, and Kyla thought she saw him nod. 'It's about yesterday. . .'

Kyla's foot stilled. 'Yesterday? At the hospital, you mean?' A shiver of apprehension licked her spine.

'Kyla, I'm sorry.' Nairne reached for Kyla and pulled her into a warm hug, the unexpectedness of the gesture making Kyla gasp. She closed her eyes as the distinctive floral perfume enfolded her, and couldn't help wondering if she was dreaming. She barely had time to collect her thoughts before Nairne stepped back and, putting a hand on Adam's arm, smiled up into his face.

'Adam made me see how. . .how selfish I'd been. No——' she shook her head as Adam made a protesting sound '——I know that wasn't the word you used, but that's how I see it now.'

Kyla felt a glow curl around her heart as Nairne turned to her and went on warmly, 'I understand now why you should have been the one to help Dad. Apart from the fact that you're the elder daughter, you've been away a long time and deserved a chance to make it up to Dad.'

She clapped her hands and laughed delightedly. 'There, Adam, I've apologised. It wasn't as hard as I expected.' Her blue eyes glowed like pansies in sunlight. 'And I feel much better.'

Kyla looked at Adam, her quick glance sending a message of gratitude. And in that glance, swift though it was, he sent her a message in return. A message that created a bond between them. They both wanted Nairne to be happy, and they had both done their share this time to see that she was.

'Oh, Nairne.' Kyla felt a surge of joy. 'I'm sorry, too—sorry if you misunderstood. . .'

For the first time since her return, she could feel no animosity in the atmosphere. Kevin had snuggled up against her again, his hand slipping into hers. She had an overwhelming feeling that it *was* good to be back, that indeed, given time, things were going to turn out all right.

'Let's go, Mom.'

'All right, scallywag.' She knew the smile on her lips was repeated in her eyes as she said, 'It was good to see you both. We'll go and visit Dad now.'

'Be prepared,' warned Adam gruffly. 'Kate's in fine form again. Now that Mac's on the mend, she's busy making plans for the best family Christmas Tigh Na Mara has ever known!'

Kyla grimaced. 'What does she have in mind?'

'Well, first of all, Christmas Eve. She's going to throw a big party, with all of us, and Rory, and——'

'Oh, dear!' Kyla bit into her lower lip. 'I'm afraid I'm going to have to disappoint her there.'

'Why?' A gust of wind snatched at Nairne's hair, and

she brushed it off her face impatiently. 'Have you made plans already?'

'Honey, let me see if you can run up the steps and count them. . .' Kyla gave Kevin a pat on the shoulder, and he ran across the gravel and started hopping up and down the steps. She turned to Nairne and Adam, a frown crinkling her brow. 'Drew and I started a tradition on Christmas Eve. . .we promised we'd always stay at home, trim the tree, and have a quiet family evening, with Kevin.' Her voice shook a little as she went on, 'Even though Drew's not here any more, I still feel. . .Oh, I'm sorry.' She cleared the huskiness from her throat. 'It's just that Kevin's looking forward to it, and. . .'

As she glanced at Adam, she was jolted by the expression on his face. There was sympathy there, and also understanding, but in his grey eyes she thought she saw something else, something much harder to identify. They had a bruised, tormented look, as if he had been hurt by something she had said, wounded by her talk of her family life with Drew. But that was ridiculous. Why would that hurt him? She must be mistaken. He was in love with Nairne, and her well-being was the most important thing in the world to him. He had made that quite plain.

'Mom, six steps.' Kevin was jumping up and down in front of her. How long had he been there, waiting for her to notice him, waiting for her to emerge from her world of dreams?

Nairne filled the gap caused by Kyla's silence. 'I hear you and your mom are going to spend Christmas Eve at Glencraig House. But you'll come to Tigh Na Mara next day for Christmas dinner, won't you?'

Though the question was directed at Kevin, Kyla knew that she was the one who was going to have to answer.

'We'd love to, wouldn't we, Kev?' She tilted the brim of his sou'wester so she could see his hazel eyes.

'Is Adam coming?'

'Yes, Kevin, I'll be there.' Adam threw him a reassuring smile. 'That's a date.'

They parted on a flurry of goodbyes, and as she and Kevin walked up the steps she heard Adam and Nairne's feet crunching on the gravelled driveway. She didn't look back, but she knew Kevin's head was twisted round, knew his hazel eyes watched Adam till she pushed open the heavy door and guided him gently into the reception area.

How strange it was, she reflected as their boots clip-clopped along the long tiled corridor, that her attempts to repair her relationship with Nairne and Adam had taken such a sudden and dramatic turn for the better— and all because last night she had revealed part of the secret that had propelled her into exile in the first place! Now she and Adam were acting together to protect Nairne.

As she walked through the open doorway of Mac's ward, she saw Kate sitting by his bedside. Her father's bearded face broke into a smile when he recognised his visitors, but even as Kyla's lips curved in response she couldn't dismiss a disturbing thought that had mercilessly insinuated itself into her mind: what would Adam have done five years ago if she had revealed the whole truth to him then? Knowing the price that they would have had to pay, would *he* have decided, as Kyla had done, that Nairne must be protected. . .*at any cost*?

Mac's cheery voice broke in on her wistful wondering.

'Hello, lass. Dr Stuart tells me you and Nairne were falling over each other yesterday to give me blood!' He raised his bandaged head from his pillow and held out a hand in greeting. 'I'm a lucky man,' he boasted cheerfully, as Kyla bent to kiss his brow. 'I've got two *grand* daughters.'

Kyla straightened, and found herself staring straight into the shining depths of her mother's luminous brown eyes.

'Yes, Mac.' Kate's voice was warm and steady as she reached over and touched Kyla's cheek gently. 'Yes, Mac, indeed you do. Two *wonderful* daughters.'

CHAPTER TEN

'Look what Martha found in the attic, Mom! She says there might be a picture of my daddy in it!'

Kyla gave a last glance at her reflection in the hallstand mirror, smoothing one hand over her carefully coiled chignon before turning round. Kevin was half-way down the staircase, hanging on to the banister with one hand, flourishing a small leather-bound photograph album in the other.

'Where's your duffel coat, sweetheart? Go back upstairs and put it on. I told you we were going out——'

'Do I have to come? I want to stay with Martha. She's going to finish packing all Grandad's suits for the jumble sale, then——'

'We've been stuck in the house for days. I want you to get some fresh air now that the cold snap's finally past and the sun's shining.' When she saw the beginnings of a mutinous frown, she said in an offhand teasing tone, 'Oh, well, if you won't come, then Adam will have to cut down our Christmas tree all by himself. Pity.' She looked meaningfully at her watch. 'He and Nairne were going to pick us up in a couple of minutes—and after we cut down the tree, we were planning on going over to Tigh Na Mara to visit Grandad. He——'

Kyla chuckled as Kevin interrupted her with a loud whoop of delight. Hazel eyes shining, he tore back upstairs calling, 'Sorry, Martha, I can't help you. Me and Adam are gonna chop down the Christmas tree!'

With a fond smile, Kyla wandered through to the drawing-room. Nairne had phoned the previous evening to suggest the outing, but, suspecting that Kevin might become over-excited if he knew ahead of time, Kyla had decided not to tell him till the very last minute.

Absently she bent to pick up a Christmas card which had fallen from the mantelpiece—her parents' card, with Kate's original sketch of Tigh Na Mara on thick cream paper. What a blessing, she thought, as she propped it back by the clock, that Mac had been released from hospital two days after his accident. Immediately afterwards, the weather had changed. With the appearance of a new moon, a bitter frost had locked the countryside in an iron grip, transforming the snow-packed roads to a treacherous sheet of ice. Driving down the hill from Glencraig House had been out of the question. But though the enforced isolation had given Kyla time to help Martha with the sorting and packing of Barclay's things, and time to get used to living in her new home, it seemed that there would never be enough time to permit her to strengthen the defensive shield round her heart.

'I'm ready Mom.'

Kevin stood in the doorway, the bone toggles of his grey duffel coat fastened, and a red wool toque pulled lop-sidedly over his ears. Red-mittened hands clutched the photo album to his chest.

'Sweetheart, you can't take——' Kyla uttered an exclamation of dismay as she heard the strident sound of a car horn. 'There they go!' Perhaps it would have been better if, like Kevin, she hadn't known in advance about the outing. All morning she had been trying to keep her emotions on an even keel, but now, just knowing that Adam would be waiting outside with Nairne, she felt all her resolutions to be calm swiftly dissipate. She hurried over to Kevin and took the album.

'Let's leave it here, and you can look at it when you get back.' Without giving him time to argue, she tossed it on to the coffee-table, and ushered him to the foot of the stairs.

With fingers that trembled a little, she turned up the collar of her burgundy jacket. 'We're off, Martha!' Her voice echoed breathlessly up the stairwell, and almost immediately Martha appeared above them on the landing.

'Lunch at one, and it's roast beef. Dinna be late,' she added tartly, swishing her feather duster warningly through the air like a whip, 'or the Yorkshire pudding will be as tough as old boots.'

As Kyla shut the front door, she could hear Kevin chant under his breath, 'Tough as old boots, tough as old boots,' but all her attention was concentrated on the sight that met her eyes. It was no surprise to see the Rover, because Nairne's red Morris was too small to carry a tree; and it was no surprise to see Adam uncoiling himself from the driver's seat of his car. . .

What did surprise—and dismay—her was that Nairne wasn't with him.

He had come alone.

'This one, this one!'

Kevin's excited shout echoed down the wooded hillside as he skipped around a six-foot high fir tree. Adam had parked the car by the side of the road, and he and Kyla had strolled along the path in the woods while Kevin ran ahead. Weak winter sunlight filtered through the evergreens, endowing the sombre atmosphere with an ethereal emerald glow.

'This is the one, is it?' Adam cast an experienced eye over the tree. 'Good lad! You've picked a topper. Just the right height and the right shape.'

Kyla saw a blush of pleasure colour Kevin's cheeks as Adam wielded his axe. What a wonderful way he had with children, she thought. He seemed so comfortable with Kevin. Did he feel as comfortable with her, or was he as ill at ease as she was? she wondered. Did he feel the chemistry she sensed between them? Did he have to jam his hands into his pockets to keep from touching her, as she did when she looked at the dark hair curling over the collar of his black turtle-neck?

Oh, she must stop thinking that way——

'How long now till Christmas Eve, Mom?'

Kyla looked down at Kevin, thankful to have her wistful introspection interrupted. 'Only two more days,' she murmured automatically.

One red-mittened hand beckoned her to lean down, and as she crouched beside him he pulled her head close to his. She felt his lips warm against her ear. 'Can he come and help us trim the tree?'

Kevin kicked impatiently at the ground, waiting for Kyla's answer, and the smell of rotting pine needles rose to fill her nostrils. She sensed that Adam had paused, and was glad that Kevin had spoken so quietly.

'I'm afraid not, sweetheart,' she murmured, tweaking Kevin's lop-sided toque into place before giving him a hug. 'Adam has other plans for Christmas Eve. He won't have time to——'

'I've got time, Kyla.'

Kyla jerked upright as Adam's deep voice reverberated in the stillness of the woods. She felt her face pale as he said, 'You're not forgetting what we agreed on a couple of weeks ago? That Sunday evening?' His eyes finished the sentence for him, sending the words he couldn't say in front of Kevin: *in the kitchen, after Kevin's nightmare, when you asked me to be there for him, as long as he needed me?*

'But Kate's plans for——'

'I'll go there later. That won't be a problem. Unless,' there was a flash of steel as he lifted the axe and absently tested the blade against the pad of one thumb, 'my joining you on Christmas Eve will be a problem for *you*?'

His gaze pinned her so that she couldn't look away. 'No, of course not. Why should it be a problem for me?' She managed to inject a touch of nonchalance into her voice. 'Kevin and I would love you to come over, even for a little while. Would six-thirty be too early for you?'

'Six-thirty's fine.'

Kyla watched with a tight smile on her lips as Kevin dashed headlong along the path after some small creature that had scurried by. His 'Yeah, Adam's coming!' rang through the trees as he disappeared from view.

In the sudden hush that followed, Kyla was very conscious that she and Adam were alone. She could feel the tension, almost hear it, vibrating and twanging in the space between them.

'You said in the car that Nairne and Rory had to go out on a case?' Would Adam guess that she had brought Nairne's name into the conversation in an effort to bring her between them, if only in spirit?

If he did, he gave no clue in his laconic response. 'Yes, they had a call from one of the lads they work with.'

'On a Saturday?' Kyla couldn't hide her surprise.

Adam laughed, standing back as the tree fell with a whoosh. 'Those two don't give a damn what time of the day or night it is, far less what day of the week, when it comes to their work. Sometimes they stay up half the night.'

'And that doesn't bother you?' Oh, why did I say that? Kyla bit hard into her lip, but it was too late.

Adam bent to hack off a couple of the lower branches. 'Bother me? Why should it?'

'Oh, I don't know. . .' Kyla waved to Kevin as he reappeared. 'I guess. . .I was thinking that after you're married, you wouldn't want her to be out late at night. . .' Her voice trailed away as horror filled her. How had she managed to get on to this topic? Why was she talking about their marriage, and what their nights would be like?

Adam grasped the rough trunk of the tree in one hand and the shaft of the axe in the other. As he watched Kevin scoot past to run ahead of them once again, shouting at the top of his voice, 'Tough as old boots, tough as old boots,' he said softly,

'I've never been married before. You have more experience than I have.' He pulled the tree behind him, and its branches made a scratching noise on the path as he trailed it across a patch of ice. 'What do *you* think?' One of his brows rose in arrogant demand. '*Should* it bother me?'

Kyla felt an ache in her throat as she stared up through the twined boughs forming an intricate arch above them. 'I. . .I don't know enough about your relationship with Nairne to. . .to be able to answer that.'

They had reached the fringe of the forest, and Kevin hopped impatiently by the Rover.

Kyla saw Adam's neck muscles tighten as he turned to look at her. 'I trust Nairne. As far as I'm concerned, she could stay out all night with Rory——' his voice was even and impassive '——and I wouldn't miss a wink of sleep.'

He hoisted the tree on to the roof-rack of the Rover and secured it with a length of binder twine. When he opened the car door Kevin scrambled in first, and as Kyla brushed past him he detained her, his hand circling her wrist. Startled, she glanced up and felt her eyes widen in dismay when she saw the haunted expression on his face. His skin had a grey tinge, the lines grooving his cheeks harsh and implacable.

'Trust.' She felt his fingers tighten like a noose of steel around her fragile bones. 'Trust is the basis of my relationship with your sister, Kyla. And trust is going to be the cornerstone of our marriage.'

She stood looking up at him breathlessly, seconds stretching like hours. At last she slid her gaze away, unable to meet the accusation implicit in his expression, and as she did he removed his hand. Expelling her breath, she drew her jacket around her and slipped past him, sliding on to the seat as he slammed the door.

She didn't dare look at him as he lowered his muscular frame into the driver's seat. She was afraid that he might look into her eyes, and see the yearning for him that was tearing her apart.

'I've heard of last-minute Christmas shopping, but this is ridiculous!' Alex Gordon's lips drew back in an unctuous smile as he scanned Kyla's signature on the forms she'd just slid back across his desk.

The irony in the lawyer's voice wasn't lost on Kyla. Buying a large estate like Bruach wasn't something one did everyday, particularly the day before Christmas, a time when the housing market was flat.

'Thanks for your co-operation, Alex.' She stood up, rubbing the muscles knotted at her neck. 'It was important to me to close the deal before the holidays.'

'And you've made up your mind to sell Ferguson Whisky?' Alex sauntered lazily round the desk to lift Kyla's sable coat from the leather sofa and hold it out for her.

'Yes.' Kyla shrugged her arms into the silk-lined sleeves. 'I've given it a lot of thought. . .'

'You must be finding it lonely at the big house with just Martha for company, my dear. And missing your late husband, too, I expect. If you need any-thing. . .*anything at all*. . .over the festive season, just give me a call, and I'd be delighted to drive over. . .'

Kyla had bent over to pick up her handbag from the chair. The silky hairs at her nape bristled warningly as a stealthy hand followed the curve of her hip, and skimmed over her buttock.

She stifled a horrified gasp and smoothly stepped away from him. He had slid his hands innocently into the pockets of his black pin-striped jacket, but his brown eyes glittered lasciviously.

Kyla tucked her bag under her arm and flashed him a

diamond-hard smile. 'That's very kind of you, Alex. Let me check my calendar, and I'll get back to you. . .'

Walking to the door, she continued in a voice that was frosted with icy spicules, 'I'd love to have you and Mrs Gordon over. I haven't seen her since I came back to the glen, and I'm sure we'd have so much to tell each other. . .'

She twisted the doorknob and turned to face him. 'Oh, one last thing, Alex. I know that Barclay thought very highly of you; however, when I sell Ferguson Whisky, I may look for a lawyer in the city—probably in one of the large Aberdeen firms. I'll have a lot of money to invest, and I'll need someone to advise me. Someone whom I can. . .*trust*.' When she noticed the perspiration that suddenly beaded his oily face, she was almost ashamed of her deliberately callous ultimatum, veiled though it was. Almost. She pulled the door open. 'You do understand?'

The lawyer took a white handkerchief from his breast pocket, and flapping it open wiped his brow. The lecherous gleam had disappeared like magic from his eyes; they were all at once as wide and subservient as any lap-dog's. Greed, Kyla acknowledged with a thankful sigh, was stronger than lust. . .at least, in Alex Gordon's book.

'Perfectly.' He dabbed at his upper lip. 'Rest assured, Mrs Ferguson, you can have implicit faith in me.'

His ingratiating, 'Have a Merry Christmas!' followed her as she clattered down the wooden stairs, but as soon as she stepped out on to the pavement she shoved him out of her mind.

It was Christmas Eve, and her spirits rose despite herself. A cold breeze blew her hair across her cheeks, bringing with it the tantalising smell of fish and chips from the take-away round the corner. She couldn't help smiling as elation spilled over in her heart. She had bought Bruach. . .she could hardly wait to tell Nairne tomorrow over Christmas dinner at Tigh Na Mara. . .

But tonight all her attention was going to be focused on Kevin. He had gone for a long nap after lunch as he wanted to stay up in the evening; they were going to trim the tree after dinner.

It was an event to which they were both looking forward. But as she crossed the street to the Bentley she had to admit that the knowledge that Adam was going to join in had blunted the edge of her own joyful anticipation.

'Martha, I thought you said the Christmas decorations were in the boxroom. I can't find——'

Kyla was half-way into the kitchen before she realised the housekeeper wasn't there. She raised her eyebrows. The door of the dishwasher lay open, the sink was filled with soapy water and pans. Strange, she mused; she could have sworn she'd heard the clink of china.

As she turned away, something caught her attention and she paused, alarm prickling at her nape. Was that *smoke* wisping from behind the closed door of the broom cupboard? Surely not. . .

She took a step closer, thinking her eyes must be playing tricks on her. And then she smelled it—smelled something burning. Oh, heavens! she thought anxiously. What am I supposed to do now? She knew that when there was a fire you shouldn't open doors—but, if she didn't look into the cupboard, how would she know how serious the situation was?

'Martha,' she shouted, '*Martha*! Where are you? The house is on fire!'

The hysterical sound had barely vibrated back from the ceiling when the cupboard door burst open with a force that made Kyla squeal with fright. She stared incredulously as a black-cardiganed figure lurched into the room, enveloped in a cloud of tobacco smoke and accompanied by the clatter of brooms, mops and dustpan.

'Where?' Ignoring the half-smoked cigarette in her hand, Martha whirled round and round, her sharp green eyes darting everywhere. 'Landsakes, missy, where is it? Why are you standing there like a stook of hay if the place is burning?'

Kyla leaned helplessly against the table, fighting an eruption of laughter. No fire after all; just Martha jumping into the cupboard with her cigarette when she'd heard her mistress coming! She mustn't let the old biddy know she saw the funny side of it, or she'd never be able to enforce her no-smoking rule. . .

Pressing her knuckles against her mouth, she made for the door. 'I'm sorry, Martha. I guess I. . .I was mistaken. It was just the smell of your cigarette smoke. . .'

Slamming the door shut, she gave way to a fit of the giggles as she crossed the hall. When she was only half-way to the drawing-room, she heard someone ring the front door bell.

Her chuckles died in her throat; she didn't need to glance at her watch to realise that it must be Adam. Hurrying to the hallstand to wipe her tear-stained face at the mirror, she was taken aback at the sight of her sparkling eyes, her pink cheeks. Perhaps it was true that laughter was the best medicine, she thought ruefully; she hadn't looked so well for a long time. . .nor, she admitted reluctantly, so attractive. Her cream tussore blouse with its pearl-buttoned cuffs and high lace collar was a perfect foil for her long black velvet skirt.

Adam was standing on the stoop when she opened the door, his face half turned away. The light from the hall fell on his strong, craggy profile, and the night shadows made him look stern and forbidding.

'Come in, Adam.' Kyla caught a whiff of whisky on his breath as he walked by her, and she guessed that he had joined the distillery staff in a Christmas dram. 'Let me take your coat.'

'Thanks.' Adam rubbed his hands together as she turned to the hallstand. 'It's raw outside. The roads are clear, though.' She swivelled round to find that he was scrutinising her; he immediately shuttered his eyes, but not in time to conceal the naked admiration that had been revealed in their grey depths. 'You're looking well, Kyla.' His expression was bland, his voice impersonal. 'Better than you were when you first came back.'

Kyla firmly dismissed the quick leap of her pulse. 'You're looking well yourself, Adam. That's a smart blazer.' She cursed the narrowness of her skirt as she walked past him, her normal energetic stride restricted to a sexy sashay.

'Kevin's waiting in here.' She halted outside the drawing-room. 'I'll get the decorations. Martha. . .' a stray giggle threatened to erupt and she choked it back before going on, 'Martha says they're in the boxroom, but I can't find them. I'll be back in a minute. . .'

She pushed open the door. Kevin was lying on the carpet, beside the tree, engrossed in the little photograph album Martha had given him a couple of days before. He'd been carting it about everywhere, Kyla mused absently. She must take a few minutes to glance at it herself some time. It looked like a family heirloom; what was he finding that was so fascinating?

'Guess who's here?' She stepped back to let Adam walk by, and when she saw Kevin's eyes light up, saw Adam hold out his arms, her emotions churned in a tormented bittersweet tangle. Kevin leaped to his feet, photograph album forgotten.

'Adam, Adam. . .' His red overalls were a bright flash of colour as he charged across the room. Kyla closed the door as Adam swept up the small figure and swung him to the ceiling. Pausing at the foot of the stairs, she leaned against the newel post, trying to control her erratic pulse, trying to recapture the gaiety she'd felt when Martha had catapulted out of the broom cupboard.

It was impossible. She hitched up the hem of her skirt and made for the kitchen. Loving Drew had been so much easier than being in love with Adam, she reflected miserably. In her marriage she'd known none of the emotional ups and downs that characterised this other relationship.

Now Adam was going to be her brother-in-law. How was one supposed to feel about one's sister's husband?

Certainly not the way she felt about Adam, she told herself angrily as she slammed into the kitchen. But, try as she would, there waas nothing she could do about it!

'Here, Adam, I found it! I knew that Grandad would have an angel or a star!' Kevin held up a delicate white and gold angel, with tinselled wings and a miniature halo. 'Can you put it on top of the tree?'

Adam threw another log on the fire and replaced the fire guard. Brushing his hands on the seat of his grey flannels, he drawled. 'That's a job for the lady of the house, I think.' He looked down at Kyla, who was sitting on the carpet, her back against the edge of the sofa. 'If you've finished organising the empty boxes, why don't you get up and do some real work?'

Kyla heard Kevin titter as she tried to get up gracefully, only to find herself hobbled by her tight skirt. She felt herself grow warm with embarrassment as she realised she couldn't get to her feet unless she pulled the fabric up to her thighs.

'Your mother's stuck, Kev. I'm afraid she may never stand again.'

Kyla looked up to see Adam looming above her, a mocking smile on his face. Though the room was large and spacious, she had been feeling claustrophobic ever since she'd come down with the boxes of decorations. She found Adam's presence overwhelming, found it impossible to keep her eyes off him. She had watched him as he helped Kevin with the tree, watched him as he bent to throw a log in the fire, watched him as he brushed his hands against his flannels. What was the matter with her? Usually she had more self-control.

With a great effort, she forced a smile. 'Give me a hand, then!'

'Shall I help her, Kevin?'

Kevin didn't answer. He had crawled over to the tree, and was trying to fix the angel to one of the lower branches.

'OK.' Adam stretched out both hands to Kyla. 'Up you come.'

For a full five seconds Kyla hesitated. Faced with the choice of revealing the full length of her nylon-sheathed legs or grasping Adam's hands, she couldn't make up her mind what to do. Finally, with a defeated sigh, she held out her hands. She bit her lip as she felt the firm warmth of Adam's fingers, and then he tugged her up, and she found herself stumbling gracelessly against his chest.

As he steadied her she stiffened, and with a breathless, 'Thanks,' tried to extricate herself, but he didn't let her go. Not right away. As he'd pulled her up, he had slid his arms round her back to catch her. Now she was captured, her breasts pressing against the lapels of his blazer. The embrace was so sudden, so unexpected, that a tiny moan escaped her lips. But when she jerked her head up to protest the words died in her throat. Adam didn't have time to hide the agonised, yearning look in his eyes. She felt him tremble, felt her eyelids close as the ache of longing in her own heart became an unbearable pain. His lips brushed over her forehead, touched her eyelids in feather-light kisses.

'Oh, Adam. . .' She felt all her resolve drain away as she let herself slump against him. How could she fight this attraction that exploded when they touched? She didn't have the strength, and right now she didn't even have the will. Even with her eyes shut, she was acutely aware of everything about him. . .the male, earthy smell of his skin that mingled with the smell of whisky, the wild beat of his heart, the searing touch of his lips as they renewed their old familiarity with the curve of her cheek, the planes of her temples. 'We mustn't,' she whispered, her voice thin and tortured.

She heard Adam's groan as he pulled her even closer, and felt an answering, involuntary response in her own body as she felt the hard arousal of his. But at the same time her mind conjured up a picture of Nairne, a picture of Nairne standing like this with Adam, provoking the same desire as she herself was provoking now. . .

She felt again the now-familiar surge of jealousy. It slashed through her, and the hurt was enough to bring her to her senses. 'Stop it,' she begged, 'let me go.'

Tearing herself out of his arms, she stood back, her breath ragged and distressed. Kevin was still playing by the tree, with his back to them, and had noticed nothing of the incident. Thank goodness, Kyla thought; he was just at the age when he might innocently say the wrong thing at the wrong moment. She didn't look at Adam as she smoothed down her blouse and ordered her tembling legs to take her over to Kevin.

'Honey,' she said, 'give me the angel. I'll show you where it should go.'

She was intensely aware of Adam's eyes on her as she stood on her tiptoes and fixed the angel to the tip of the tree. Swallowing to relieve the tightness of her throat, she stood back. She had to get rid of Adam. She couldn't stand it any longer: to be so close to him, but not to be his. . .

'You can have hot chocolate and cookies, Kevin, and then it's bedtime.' She glanced at her watch, avoiding looking at Adam. 'It was awfully good of you to come and help us, Adam. I. . .I guess you'll have to go now.'

'Don't go, Adam.' Kevin stuck his hands in his overall pockets, imitating Adam's casual stance. 'I want a bed-time story.'

'Adam doesn't have——'

'Time? I've got the time, Kyla.' At last Kyla let her eyes dart over to him, and she found him staring at her impassively, nothing in his manner revealing that moments before his body had revealed how much he wanted her. 'I'll read him a story, and then let's *all* have a snack!'

'Oh.' Kyla tried to gather her senses together. 'No, his books are upstairs. I——'

'I want Adam to read this book to me, Mom.' Kevin crawled under the tree and retrieved his photograph album.

Kyla flashed Adam a tight smile. 'It's a photograph album that Martha unearthed—it looks as if it's a hundred years old, but if that's what he wants. . .' She shrugged her shoulders.

'Great. Come and sit on my knee over here on the sofa.' Adam threw off his blazer and slackened the knot of his maroon and silver tie. Kyla turned away quickly, wishing that he had kept on the blazer. The more clothes he had on, the more comfortable she felt.

'I'll get the cocoa and cookies,' she murmured as she walked to the door. But they weren't listening. Already Kevin was on Adam's knee, already she could hear Adam's warm baritone voice saying, 'Once upon a time, there was a family whose name was Ferguson. . .'

'Here we are, cocoa and cookies for three,' Kyla called with an attempt at cheerfulness for Kevin's sake as she kicked the door shut behind her. 'Sorry I was so long, but I was chatting with Martha.' Briefly she thought about their little talk. They had come to an agreement: the housekeeper could smoke in her own room any time she wanted; she could smoke in the kitchen only in the evenings after Kevin had gone to bed. 'Story almost finished?'

'We're just coming to the last page.' Adam glanced up and jerked his head towards the figure curled up in his lap. 'Someone's almost asleep,' he added.

'I'm not, Adam.' Thickly lashed eyelids drooped over hazel eyes. 'Show me the picture of Auntie Nairne.'

'Nairne?' Kyla's fingers paused for a moment as she laid down the tray. Absently picking up a tea biscuit, she moved to perch on one arm of the sofa. 'Where is it, Adam?'

'We haven't come to it yet.'

'It's on the last page,' Kevin murmured sleepily. 'She's wearing a funny hat and dress. . .but it's Auntie Nairne.' He yawned, and Kyla smiled as his eyes closed.

The album was old, with stiff black pages. The photographs had obviously been taken many years ago; they were faded and sepia-toned. Under each one was written a name, a date, a location.

Kyla nibbled on the edge of her biscuit as Adam turned to the last page. It held only one photo, a portrait of a young woman, which someone had tinted by hand. As Kyla looked at it, she felt a slow numbness creep over her mind, but despite the numbness she was certain of one thing: Kevin was wrong in thinking the picture was of Nairne. . .it had obviously been taken many years before she was born.

But Kyla wasn't surprised that he had thought it was his aunt. Though a cloche cupped the head of the woman in the picture, her hair was identical to Nairne's—long, reddish-fair, wavy. And their features were so alike, they could have been twins. Large blue eyes looked gravely into the camera, fine, intelligent features were beautiful even in repose.

Horror strangled the words of protest in Kyla's throat as the implication of what she was seeing jostled aside every other thought in her head. Oh, if only she'd taken the time to sit with Kevin some time during the last two days and look at the album! Now it was too late. Her eyes blurred with futile tears as she read the inscription written in a scrawling hand below the photo: Andrewina Ferguson, Glencraig House, nineteen hundred and seven.

Drew's grandmother? His great-grandmother? Kyla's mind was in too much of a turmoil to figure it out. Out of the corner of her eye she saw Adam's shoulders gradually stiffen. Apprehension tingled its way along her spine as the atmosphere in the room shifted and changed with the unpredictable, staggering intensity of an earthquake.

She saw the tremor that shook Adam's fingers as he closed the album and put it down. Kevin didn't stir as strong arms lifted him gently and carried him to the door.

Adam's step on the stair wasn't as firm as usual, nor as confident. Listening to it, Kyla thought it sounded like the step of a much older man.

Her body felt chilled and damp as she hugged her arms against her chest. How much of the truth had Adam guessed?

She stared into the leaping yellow flames in the fire and waited for him to come back.

CHAPTER ELEVEN

'OCH, ye're still here! I thought I heard you go upstairs.'

Kyla twisted round with a startled gasp as she heard Martha's voice behind her. So intently had she been listening for the sound of Adam's heavy brogues on the stairs, she hadn't heard the housekeeper's slippered feet.

'No, it was Adam.' She inhaled a steadying breath. 'He's putting Kevin to bed.'

'I'm for bed too as soon as I put these mugs in the dishwasher.' Glancing at the now-cold cocoa, the housekeeper picked up the tray and shuffled away from the coffee-table. 'I'll see you in the morning.'

Kyla half turned to say 'goodnight', but as she parted her lips she caught a glimpse of Adam in the doorway, and a chill of foreboding shivered down her spine. His face was pale and drawn, his black hair dishevelled as if he had run his fingers through it over and over again in the last few minutes.

'The tree looks bonny.' Martha flung the comment over her shoulder as Adam stepped aside to let her past.

'Aye, it does.' His gaze was clamped relentlessly on Kyla as he uttered the mechanical response, 'Goodnight, Martha.' Closing the door, he leaned back against it, his body rigid.

Time ceased to have any meaning for Kyla as silence throbbed thickly between them. If she'd had any doubts as to whether Adam had finally put the pieces of the puzzle together, the stark look in his eyes shattered them. When at length his harsh voice rasped into the quietness, she felt herself tumbling into space, knowing there was no safety net to catch her.

'You've known all along, haven't you?'

A sigh of utter weariness escaped her as she listened to the lead-heavy tone of his words. The deception was finally over—at least as far as Adam was concerned. When she had opened her Pandora's box to let the first secret out, all the others had escaped with it, despite her efforts to recapture them. She lifted the cushion from her chair and hugged it apprehensively against her pounding heart as Adam jerked away from the door and started towards her.

It was obvious that, though he had guessed the truth, he wasn't going to rest till he heard it from her own lips. Why was her throat clogged with emotion, why was she feeling so dizzy and helpless? Was it because, if she answered his question in the affirmative, it would be all too obvious to Adam that she had never stopped loving him?

There was little comfort in the plump red cushion as she curled her fingers into its velvety softness. 'Yes,' she whispered, when she could bear the menacing silence no longer. 'I have. Just after Drew proposed to Nairne. . .I. . .I. . .overheard a conversation between Kate and Barclay, and learned that Barclay was Nairne's father.'

She jumped as Adam's uncontrolled savage oath exploded into the room. 'Why the *hell* didn't you tell me?'

Tears pricked Kyla's eyes and the cushion tumbled to the floor as she got up and walked blindly to the window. Pulling aside the heavy curtain, she rested her watery gaze on the darkness outside, darkness broken only by scattered sequins of light pinpointing the houses along the glen. Homes filled with people enjoying Christmas Eve together, she thought bleakly, families who were able to put aside their everyday cares in this festive season. Oh, why could she not be one of them? she wondered. Why could *her* cares not be simple and everyday?

'Nairne had to be protected, and I was the only one who could do anything.' She watched numbly as her unsteady breath drifted a veil of mist over the cold pane. 'I'm sure you remember how immature she was at seventeen—immature, idealistic and naïve. I had to make a decision: whether it would be harder for her to handle the knowledge that she had been in love with her half-brother for as long as she could remember, that Kate had committed adultery and Mac wasn't her real father——'

'Or?'

Kyla's heart gave a violent lurch as Adam's grim voice sounded right behind her. 'Or,' she went on tremulously, 'to cope with betrayal by her sister and her fiancé. I decided that she'd be devastated if Drew and I eloped. . .but I was convinced that if she found out the truth about her relationship with Drew, *it would totally destroy her*. I wasn't willing to take that chance. . .'

Her words jerked to a halt as Adam grasped her shoulders, and her body stiffened defensively as he slowly turned her round to face him.

'So you lied when you said you were in love with Drew?'

Kyla felt a relentless ache behind her breastbone as she met his hard, inscrutable gaze. 'Yes.' Again she whispered. 'I lied.'

She saw his eyelids flicker. 'And you lied when you said you'd stopped loving me?'

For an endless moment, Kyla stared beseechingly into eyes that gave no quarter. Then, to her dismay, she felt a tear trickle down her cheek. As she clumsily brushed it aside, she felt others take its place, and all at once it was as if a dam had burst. The unhappiness she'd kept bottled up for the past five years surged uncontrollably to the surface. Hot tears burned her eyes, welling over to run down her cheeks and splash on to her silk blouse, but she was past caring. The pain of loving Adam, the pain of knowing she could never have him, was suddenly more than she could bear.

'Yes,' she cried despairingly, 'yes, that was a lie. It was all lies. I lied when I said I'd fallen in love with Drew, I lied when I said I'd stopped loving you. I've *never* stopped loving you. I loved you then, I love you now, I'll probably go to my grave loving you. . .' A choking little sob escaped her trembling lips. 'And I'm sorry if it causes you embarrassment, that your future sister-in-law is in love with you. . .'

Wildly she tugged aside the thick strands of hair that were sticking to her damp cheeks and looked up at Adam, but even through the tangled wetness of her long lashes she could see a look of horror on his face that froze her breath.

'Is *that* what you think?' His voice shook with incredulity. 'Is *that* what you think I feel, now that I know the truth?' His low exclamation was loaded with self-contempt. 'I wouldn't treat a dog the way I've treated you since you came back to the glen. My behaviour. . .my cruelty. . .have been unforgivable. And yet you can say you still *care* for me?' His throat worked convulsively, and for a long, awkward moment he couldn't go on. '*Embarrassment*? Oh, dear heaven. . .'

Kyla felt herself shrink away from him in disbelief as she heard his anguished groan. There was no doubt that he was utterly torn with remorse; his defences, like her own, had crumbled, leaving him as exposed as herself. He was no longer trying to hide his emotions, and in his vulnerability he revealed without the need for words that he too had never. . .

Kyla drew in a shuddering gasp. She must be losing her mind! What on earth was she thinking? Had she been about to tell herself that Adam was still in love with her?

The air between them quivered with emotion as, despite her reluctance, Kyla's gaze was drawn again, hypnotically, into the depths of his pewter-grey eyes. She felt her body sway unsteadily. Surely it was just compassion she was seeing, she thought hysterically; anything more must be pure fantasy, a result of her mindless yearning for him. He was in love with Nairne, he was engaged to marry her. . .But she knew she had never loved him more than at this moment. More than anything in the world she wanted to reach out to him, put her arms round him, rest her head against his heart. . .

'Oh. . .' With a piteous little cry, she brushed past him, half blinded by the swathe of hair that swirled across her cheeks. As she stumbled to the door, she could hear his harsh breathing, but some innate instinct told her he wouldn't try to follow her. When she reached the top of the stairs, she crumpled to the carpet, huddling against the banisters with her face hidden in her hands as Adam's heavy step crashed across the hall.

Moments later she heard the violent slamming of the front door, and the finality of the sound reverberated in her heart.

'You'll have to put your new toys away in a few minutes, Kevin. We'll be going to Tigh Na Mara soon.' Kyla sat back on her heels in the midst of the crumpled Christmas paper strewn all over the drawing-room carpet. How was she going to get through the day without falling apart? she wondered. She felt as if she were floundering in a dark fog of depression and despair. Even seeing Kevin's happiness couldn't dispel the tears that had been lurking behind her eyelids ever since she had awakened.

'Can I take my bike with me?' Kevin brushed a hand over his flushed cheeks and fixed his mother with eager hazel eyes.

Tousling his hair, Kyla nodded and jumped to her

feet. 'Yes,' she murmured huskily, 'there's room in the boot. We——'

She heard the door open and turned. When she saw Martha, she cleared her throat. 'I thought I heard the doorbell. Has your son come to pick you up already?'

'Jack won't be here till noon. No, that was the phone you heard. Your mother wants to speak to you.' Martha began picking up the discarded paper. 'I'll keep an eye on the laddie till you get back.'

The radio was on in the kitchen, and Kyla clicked off the strains of 'Joy to the World' before sinking into the old rocker, phone at her ear. 'Merry Christmas, Kate.' With a great effort, she injected a lightness into her tone.

'Kyla!' Her mother's voice was shrill and urgent. 'There's something I have to tell you before you come over.'

'What's the matter?' Kyla gripped the handset tightly waiting for an answer. Only once before had she heard her mother so upset. . .

'After Adam left last night, and your dad went to bed, I. . .I had a talk with Nairne. I told her. . .told her that Barclay was her father.'

'Kate!' Shock and bewilderment brought Kyla to her feet again in a startled lurch. '*You promised*! When we had that talk at the hospital, we agreed to protect Nairne. We both——'

'We were wrong.' Kate's voice still shook, but she sounded adamant. 'Kyla, I've done nothing but think since. . .since I found out that you knew. And the more I thought about it, the more I realised Nairne has a right to the truth—especially now that she's engaged to be married. She and Adam will in all likelihood have children. She should know Barclay was her father. There may be times when the information may be vital to a doctor——'

Despite the warmth in the kitchen, Kyla felt goose bumps prickle over her skin. 'Dear lord, Kate. . .'

'I told her everything. I told her about Barclay coming to Tigh Na Mara after Hilda died. . .I told her I found myself pregnant, and that there was no doubt that the child was Barclay's. . .Oh, Kyla, she was devastated. Her face became deathly white. It broke my heart. She ran from the room, saying she had to tell Adam. I tried to stop her, but she wouldn't listen to me. She took the car, and I saw the lights disappear in the direction of Redhillock. And, Kyla. . .'

'Yes, Kate?' Kyla pressed the palm of her free hand against her temple in a vain attempt to stop the sudden pounding in her head.

'She didn't come home. She phoned me just now from Redhillock.'

It took several seconds for Kate's words to sink in. Kyla felt her shoulders slump as she shook her head back and forth disbelievingly. 'She stayed out all night?' A green flame of jealousy seared her as she pictured Adam comforting Nairne. Immediately it was followed by a deep feeling of shame. How could she be so self-centred at a time like this?

'Kyla, are you all right?' Kate's voice was taut.

'Yes, I'm fine.' Kyla gave a bitter smile. What did one more lie matter?

'I just wanted you to know. . .'

Kyla didn't miss the unspoken plea for reassurance underlying her mother's words. It drew a sudden surge of love for her. She took a deep breath. Whatever Kate had done in the past, and for whatever reasons, she had never meant to hurt anyone. 'Kate,' she said emphatically, 'don't worry. Everything's gong to be all right.'

Kyla's fingers trembled as she replaced the receiver. Kate would be fine, there was great stength hidden in that small, wiry body. But would Nairne be all right? Anxiety tore at Kyla, as well as a longing to see her, to comfort her.

But Nairne had Adam to comfort her, as he had been comforting her during the night.

Tears spilled down Kyla's cheeks with copious abandon as she sank back on to the old rocker. Not until this moment had she realised that somewhere in the deepest recesses of her heart she had kept alive a secret hope that somehow, some day, she and Adam would be reunited. That somewhere in the future, for them, there really would be a happy ending.

And as she wiped away her tears she knew that with them she was wiping away her dreams.

CHAPTER TWELVE

'WATCH, Mom, don't scratch it!' Kevin screwed up his face anxiously as he watched Kyla manoeuvre his brand-new bike into the Bentley's boot.

'Don't worry, I'm being careful.' Kyla scooped up the gaily wrapped Christmas packages precariously balanced in his arms. 'We haven't forgotten anyone, have we?' she asked as she tucked them in beside the bike. 'This is Grandma's, and here's Grandad's, and Nairne's——'

'And Rory's, and don't break the glasses we bought for Adam.' Kevin hopped up and down on the gravel.

'No, I——' Kyla broke off abruptly as she heard a shrill voice call her name. Turning, she saw Martha at the front door.

'Adam Garvie's on the phone.' Martha's words were carried past on the wind. 'He wants to speak to you.'

Kyla felt as if a cloud had suddenly covered the hard December sun. After the briefest hesitation, she called back, 'Tell him we're on our way to Tigh Na Mara.'

'But he says it's important!'

Waving aside Martha's response, Kyla slammed the boot and helped Kevin into the passenger seat. 'Strap yourself in, Kev.' Her words were automatic, as were her actions as she started the car and swung it along the beech-lined avenue. What on earth did Adam want that couldn't keep till he saw her? Did he want to tell her how he had spent the long, intimate hours of the night comforting Nairne?

Dear heaven, where had that malicious thought come from? Oh, how could she turn up at a Christmas party in this foul mood? She had to have time to pull herself together. . .

When she reached the foot of the hill, instead of driving alongside the loch towards Tigh Na Mara, she took a left turn and made for the distillery. It would be almost unbearable to watch Adam and Nairne together, knowing Nairne had spent the night at Redhillock. She'd drive to the dam, park there, and climb the fields one last time to the old trysting place. Christmas morning was as good a time as any, she thought with a bleak twist of her lips, to say a final goodbye to the love she and Adam had shared. . .

Kyla was glad of her sable coat and winter boots when she and Kevin reached the top of the hill. Though the sun was shining brightly and most of the snow had melted, the wind was cold. It blew her hair across her face, almost obscuring her view of Kevin as he romped in the heather.

She would never come here again. It held too many bittersweet memories. Catching the unruly strands from her cheeks, she raised her arms and pinned her hair at her nape with her hands. 'Just a few moments,' she whispered to herself, 'just a few moments to remember. . .' To remember how they had met here on summer evenings. . .

Most of the time Adam would arrive first, but once in a while she'd be there before him. On those occasions, she'd walk around impatiently, hating the wasted moments, her gaze drawn eagerly to the hillside, watching for his tall figure to appear.

Today, the dam glistened and sparkled as the wind teased its surface. She closed her eyes, remembering the happiness of bygone times, a happiness so sweet that even now she could almost taste it. A tear escaped to trickle down her cheek as she let her imagination conjure up a picture of Adam leaping up the slope towards her.

When finally she opened her eyes, she felt her heart give a great lurch. The fantasy she'd created in her mind was so vivid that for a moment she thought it was real.

She could *see* Adam striding towards her, his sheepskin jacket flapping open, his turtle-neck sweater and cords startlingly black in the sunshine. His hair was tossed in attractive disarray around his familiar features. As he drew nearer, she could see that the sharp wind—surely it was the wind?—had made his eyes glisten with tears.

'Kyla!' His voice shattered every sane thought. Her dream world and the real world slid crazily into each other, making her mind spin in dizzy circles. Hurriedly wiping her cheek with the back of her hand, she clutched her fingers together. This was no dream. Adam was really here.

He stopped in front of her, his breathing harsh and ragged. 'Thank heaven I've found you.'

Jolted by the force of her emotions, Kyla took a step back. 'Found me? What do you mean?' A mirthless smile crossed her lips. 'I didn't realise I was lost!'

'I phoned from Redhillock, but Martha said you'd already left. Then, when I got to Tigh Na Mara, you weren't there. I came to look for you.'

'There was no need.' She swung away. Hating the jealousy that twisted inside her, she tried to speak calmly. 'Kate phoned and told me what happened. She said. . .said Nairne spent the night at Redhillock. I——'

'Adam!'

Kyla jumped as Kevin interrupted her and rushed at Adam with a delighted cry. Thankful of the respite, she swallowed the painful lump in her throat as she watched Adam swing Kevin into his arms, watched Kevin's small, red-mittened hands clutch the strong, broad back of this man he adored.

'Merry Christmas, Adam.' Kevin's face was buried in the collar of Adam's jacket, his voice muffled.

'Merry Christmas to you, son.' Adam's grey gaze trapped Kyla's eyes, and before she could jerk away he had included her in their embrace. She felt his lips brush

her cheek, his breath warm and intimate, as he murmured huskily, 'And to you, Kyla, the very merriest
Christmas ever.'

Her heart ached. She knew she shouldn't let him hold
her like this, yet at his touch she felt all her resolutions
fly like straw in the wind.

'Adam, why don't you go back to Tigh Na Mara? Isn't
Nairne waiting for you?' She crushed back another surge
of jealousy as she went on, 'Or is she still at Redhillock?'

Adam acted as if he hadn't heard her. Tweaking
Kevin's toque, he said firmly, 'I want to talk to your
mother for a minute. Why don't you go and chase that
seagull?'

As Kevin ran away shouting, 'Chase that seagull. . .chase that seagull,' Kyla slid her hands into her
pockets to hide their nervous trembling. What could
Adam possibly have to say to her?

'Nairne didn't spend the night at Redhillock.'

He spoke very softly, but with an intensity that made
her pulses flutter. She compressed her lips. So Nairne
hadn't spent the night with Adam—that didn't give *her*
any reason to feel such a quick, daring relief.

'But Kate said. . .' Her protesting words faltered for
a moment as Adam moved closer. With the best will in
the world, she couldn't find the strength to push him
away when he grasped her wrists, or fight him when he
pulled her hands from her pockets to weave his fingers
through hers. Her voice was weak as she began again.
'But Kate said Nairne was going to Redhillock. . .'

Adam's fingers moved against hers with a subtle
pressure that sent a disturbing tingle of response along
her veins. 'That *was* Nairne's intention when Kate told
her that Barclay was her father, and she did set off to see
me, but on the way to Redhillock she was astounded to
find herself turning the car around, and heading in the
other direction. Kyla,' his hands clenched tightly over
hers, 'Nairne was shaken to the core when she suddenly

realised that it wasn't me she wanted to see.' He paused, and Kyla felt the tension between them tighten to breaking point. 'It was Rory.'

'Rory?' Kyla stood frozen, incredulous, not daring to believe her ears. She felt a pulse on the pad of her thumb twitch against Adam's palm. '*Rory?*'

Adam raised her hand to his mouth and touched his lips to her fingertips. 'Yes, Kyla,' his voice was a husky caress, and Kyla felt her legs begin to shake, 'not me, but Rory.'

Kyla looked up into his eyes, feeling all the blood drain from her face. She opened her mouth to speak, but the only sound that came out was a worldess squeak.

'Hush.' Adam pulled her closer. 'Let me tell you the rest. Nairne desperately needed comforting. . .and somehow, in that moment of crisis, it was to Rory that her heart led her. He took her in, and she spilled out the whole tangled story. Finally, in the early hours, she collapsed into an exhausted sleep. In the morning, she drove over to Redhillock. . .'

He paused again, this time tenderly kissing her palm before going on. 'First of all, she phoned Kate to tell her where she was, and to make her peace with her. . .And then we had a long talk. It seems,' his lips tilted in a crooked smile that set Kyla's heartbeats tumbling over each other like skittles, 'that the beautiful Drummond girls are determined to break my heart.'

Kyla felt as if her mind were a kaleidoscope, and someone had just shaken it so that all the thoughts were lying in a haphazard jumble. She knew Adam was trying to tell her something, but she couldn't quite grasp it. At least, she *thought* she knew what he meant, but it couldn't be. . .

'Yes,' he murmured, taking a strand of hair between his thumb and forefinger, 'it's what you think. Nairne came to tell me she isn't in love with me. She came to set me free.'

The invisible hand gave the kaleidoscope another almighty shake. Why didn't Adam look like a man who had just been thrown over? Kyla didn't dare acknowledge even to herself that deep inside her a tiny flame of hope was curling round her heart, warming it, making it glow. . .And she could hear music! Was it *possible*? Did skylarks sing in December?

'Oh, Adam, I'm sorry,' Kyla breathed, 'you must feel so——'

'Ecstatic? Is that the word you're searching for?' he teased her gently.

Kyla's fingers kneaded the front of his sweater, like the small paws of a kitten wanting to make contact. Everything was happening too fast. 'Adam,' she began in a tentative whisper. 'I don't understand. You asked Nairne to marry you. . .You must love her—she must have loved you, too, to accept. . .'

'We do feel love for each other, Kyla. We——'

Involuntarily Kyla tried to jerk away from Adam, but he slid his arms around her and clasped her against his chest. 'No, my darling.' She felt his fingers twine through the long, thick hair tumbling down her back. 'We care deeply for each other. . .but we've never been *in love with* each other. We became close friends when you and Drew eloped, and over the years that friendship deepened. Nairne was shattered when she heard you were coming back to Glencraig, and I asked her to marry me, believing it would help her to face you. . .and knowing I'd never be in love with anyone again after having lost you.' He slid his hands round and brushed open the front of Kyla's sable coat. 'I was pretty mixed up myself when I heard you were coming home.' His fingers moved possessively over Kyla's back till she thought her legs would buckle under her with the sheer pleasure rippling through her body. 'And until this morning, I didn't realise that subconsciously perhaps I was using Nairne to hurt you, hoping to make you feel the pain of jealousy that I felt when you married Drew. . .' His mouth twisted in a rueful smile. 'Nairne confessed this morning that she accepted my proposal because she couldn't bear to see me so unhappy, and that she thought we could make a go of marriage because we'd never know the ups and downs of an obsessive passion. . .'

'Oh, Adam.' Kyla's breath hissed out slowly. She pressed her cheek against Adam's chest, feeling the wild beat of his heart beneath the fine black wool. 'Is Nairne going to be all right?'

'She told me she cried when she realised you'd married Drew simply to remove him from her life. She considers herself lucky to have a sister who loves her so much. But you were right, Kyla, She also told me that if she'd found out the truth when she was seventeen, she would have reacted very differently from the way she has now. She might even have considered taking her own life——'

Kyla felt her lips part in horror. 'Oh, Adam, no——'

'It's all right.' He smiled. 'She's a lot stronger now than she was then.'

A frown wrinkled Kyla's brow. 'And Rory. . .Where does he fit into the picture?'

Adam chuckled. 'Rory's a confirmed bachelor. . .or so he keeps telling everyone. Truth is, he wouldn't know love if it stood up and hit him in the face. I have a strong suspicion that those two mean more to each other than they realise. But time will tell. Meantime, Nairne's going to need all our support. We'll have to make sure she doesn't have time to mope.'

Kyla opened her mouth to tell Adam about Bruach, and then closed it again with a secret smile. Plenty of time for talking later. They had so much to talk about. . .and so many decisions to make, decisions concerning Ferguson Whisky, and Alex Gordon, and Glencraig House—but they would make them together.

Later. Right now, there were more important things to do. . .

'Oh, Adam.' Kyla expelled her breath in a long ecstatic sigh. 'I do love you so. . .'

She felt his lips brush the crown of her head, felt his hands slide round her ribcage with a determination that took her breath away. Her eyes misted as his silvery eyes looked into hers with an expression of almost unbearable tenderness. 'And I love you too, my very own darling.'

Kyla's lashes, now dry of tears, feathered her flushed cheeks as she waited for Adam's kiss, a kiss she had thought was destined to be hers only in her dreams.

She heard him draw in his breath, felt his lips trace a path down her temple, over her cheek, towards the corner of her mouth——

'Adam! Adam!' Kevin's voice sounded as if it were coming from far away. 'Look what I've found!'

Adam's lips hovered over hers, she ached to feel their warm, possessive pressure——

Kevin's voice sounded again, this time far too close. . .

With a rueful smile, Adam twisted his head to look down. 'What is it, Kev?'

Kyla couldn't drag her eyes from Adam's face. What was there left to find up here? she mused dreamily. She'd already found everything that mattered!

'Heavens!' She heard Adam's low whistle, and felt a slight stirring of curiosity. What treasure had Kevin found? A sprig of white heather, a pretty chunk of granite, a silver strip of birch bark?

'Kyla——' Adam's voice was husky with emotion '—look at this!'

Tearing her eyes from her adoring appraisal of Adam's face, Kyla looked down—and gasped. For long moments, she tried to speak but couldn't. There, nestled in Adam's palm, was her engagement ring, the ring that he had flung away in anger such a long time ago. It looked as beautiful to Kyla as it had on that lovely June afternoon, even though the silver was now tarnished, and the ruby had temporarily lost its lustre.

'Oh, Adam. . .' was all she could say as he brushed the ring on his jacket and slipped it on to her slender finger. Happiness blazed through her like the searing rays of a summer sun; her dreams had really come true.

A contented sigh escaped her lips as Adam's powerful arms caught her again and pulled her hard against his lean body. She had guessed when she returned to Glencraig that the task she had set herself would bring her pain and humiliation, and she had been proved right. But she had also found out that love could survive great misfortunes.

Kevin's laughter echoed joyfully down the glen, mingling with the distant sound of Christmas bells from the Glencraig parish kirk, as Adam at last claimed Kyla's lips in a kiss that promised forever.

Harlequin Presents®

Coming Next Month

Available in January wherever paperback books are sold, or through Harlequin Reader Service:

In the U.S.
901 Fuhrmann Blvd.
P.O. Box 1397
Buffalo, N.Y. 14240-1397

In Canada
P.O. Box 603
Fort Erie, Ontario
L2A 5X3

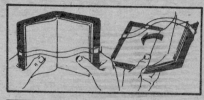

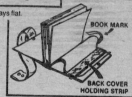